THE TYCOON
WHO HEALED
HER HEART

Staffordshire Library and Information Service

Please return or renew or by the last date shown

CHES

CHESLYN HAY

4/12

25. MAY 12

21. APR 15

21. MAY 15

8. SEP 15

18. OCT 12

08. NOV 12

12. APR 16

31/12/12

28. JAN 13

19 MAR 13

21st MAY

12.

KINVER

If not required by other readers, this item may be renewed
in person, by post or telephone, online or by email.
To renew, either the book or ticket are required

24 Hour Renewal Line
0845 33 00 740

Staffordshire
County Council

THE TYCOON WHO HEALED HER HEART

BY

MELISSA JAMES

MILLS & BOON®

First published in Great Britain 2011
by Mills & Boon, an imprint of Harlequin (UK) Limited.
Large Print edition 2012
Harlequin (UK) Limited, Eton House,
18-24 Paradise Road, Richmond, Surrey TW9 1SR

© Melissa James 2011

ISBN: 978 0 263 22573 0

Harlequin (UK) policy is to use papers that are natural,
renewable and recyclable products and made from
wood grown in sustainable forests. The logging and
manufacturing process conform to the legal environmental
regulations of the country of origin.

Printed and bound in Great Britain
by CPI Antony Rowe, Chippenham, Wiltshire

To my lovely sister CP
and confidante Mia.
We've always been there for each other,
through all the ups and downs of life.

CHAPTER ONE

Graubünden Region, Swiss Alps

'YOU'RE doing much better,' Rachel Chase's ski instructor said as he performed a smooth cross-country sliding ski across the final slope towards the Bollinger Alpine Resort.

'It's not true, Matt, but thank you for persisting with me.' With a grateful smile, Rachel filled her lungs with crisp, clean mountain air, set her jaw, turned her face and kept sliding across the baby slope. It was humiliating, but she constantly had to grab hold of his hand.

Probably she just didn't have the confidence to ski, but in every other way the Bollinger Alpine Resort had been the perfect hideout. The staff took excellent care of her in this lake-filled valley nestled beneath the Alps, and with complete discretion. When Max, the manager, had offered her refuge in a hideaway cabin at the back of the resort, she'd grabbed the chance.

For a week she'd refused to unpack, remaining ready to run again. The peace felt too good to be true after the nightmare of ringing phones and flashing cameras she'd endured in LA after Pete's lies had hit the headlines. She shuddered to think what it was like now 'Dr Pete' had discovered he could only fix his failing ratings, and hang onto the fame and adulation he craved, by publicly re-uniting with the wife he'd denounced as a cheater.

Rachel rubbed her wrist. It had long since healed, but it was symbolic. An hour after she'd seen a doctor privately and alone to have the broken limb put in a cast, she'd had the locks changed and filed for a temporary restraining-order. She hadn't pressed charges—it would have destroyed Pete—but she'd go to court if he touched her again. Her lawyer had made that crystal clear.

Her phone had been off for weeks. He couldn't use tracking, charm, love, guilt or even her mother and sister to get his way. She had enough to deal with learning how to survive alone, without the constant knowledge that her family loved Pete more than they'd ever loved her.

A soft voice asked from behind her, 'Rachel, are you okay? Does the key not work?'

She started. Though Pete had only hit her twice

before she'd left him, it had left its mark in a nervous reaction she hadn't learned to control yet. After a deep breath she turned to the pretty brunette with the hint of willowy figure that Rachel had once had to starve herself to maintain. Apart from her second cousin Suzie—who'd arranged her new name, two new passports with different names and had given her thousands of dollars Pete couldn't trace—the members of staff at Bollinger Alpine Resort were the only people she could trust.

She apologised in German and entered the cabin. 'I'm fine, thank you, Monika.' She unclipped and with both hands pulled off her snow boots and damp, tight ski socks.

Monika had brought her lunch. Jami and Max joined her soon after to listen to her stories about life as a celebrity wife in Tinsel Town. She dredged another story from the depths of all she wanted to forget for the sake of those who were risking their livelihoods to protect her.

From the corner of the *terrasse* he watched the woman holding court, three members of staff watching her in adoring awe, as if she was an affable duchess. He'd watched her trying to ski before, pretending to stumble so she could hold the hand of a young, handsome ski instructor.

He'd known women like her before and he despised them—using wiles and fame to get their way. She charmed people into falling into her hand. Obviously she revelled in being the centre of attention. And she was good at it: the sweet, rueful manner combined with her fawn-like eyes and her 'big as Texas, big as her heart' smile was a lethal cocktail for the uninitiated.

What a shame for Mrs Rachel Rinaldi—the now-infamous 'Mrs Dr Pete' of chat-show legend—that he'd been initiated into how far one could fall when the fame bubble burst. He wasn't naïve or stupid. He'd been taken, burned, lied to and left broken before she even left grade school—and he'd never let anyone do it to him since.

Mrs Rinaldi was about to discover just how far her charm would get her.

'And so He That Shall Not Be Named insisted those ten seconds of footage be cut from the interview. Apparently a top-action hero's being human enough to trip on a step and fall flat on his face could ruin his entire career and cause his wife to divorce him—quote, unquote.'

'I assume my invitation to this party was lost in the post.'

The giggles and snorts of her friends died. Brow furrowed, Rachel turned to see what was wrong, but with one look her breath caught in her lungs.

A man of dark, dangerous male beauty stood in the doorway. His tight, brooding sensuality hit her in the solar plexus like a drive-by shot. His features weren't quite classic, but his stormy eyes and sensuous mouth more than made up for the lack of perfection. His bearing had a loose-limbed elegance and his lean, strong body was encased in a dove-grey suit that complemented his eyes. She blinked hard once or twice. It felt as if the room was spinning around her—but this had happened to her once before…

I am not that girl now. She forced her eyes to remain open, focused on him. No man would ever make her close her eyes or fall to her knees again, physically or emotionally.

She held his gaze, returning it with an openness most men found unnerving. Yes, the man knew how to dress, to impress a woman with a glance, but it was probably all for show.

Definitely 'been there, done that'—and she'd thrown out the T-shirt.

'A shame, since it seems I'm the host.' The new arrival spoke quietly, but small flickers of restrained lightning showed in each word. His dark-grey eyes rested upon the occupants of the cabin one by one. And she'd thought *she* knew how to unnerve others…

'Herr Bollinger, uh, welcome back. We were not aware of your arrival.' Max spoke in German, with a nervous twitch in his left eye. Monika squirmed, and Jami gazed at the door as if it held the secrets of life.

Bollinger. So this was the resort's owner, the son of a French multi-millionaire and a French-Swiss movie star. She'd seen pictures of him from about twelve years ago, when he'd been in the top ten of the World's Beautiful People, but she'd never seen him in the flesh. Armand Bollinger—the man nicknamed 'the Wolf' for his brilliance in business circles as well as in his love life. And, now she had seen him, she knew why. The leashed storm in him took Rachel's breath anew.

He stepped inside the room, filling it with an air of absolute command, even as he spoke with exquisite courtesy. 'I'd like to speak with our guest alone, thank you.' He glanced at each of his staff in turn. Without a word, Jami, Max and Monika fled, and she couldn't blame them.

The man turned to her with a smile that was perfect, welcoming and professional. 'Ms Chase, I am Armand Bollinger.' He didn't waste words he didn't need, such as 'I am the owner of the resort'. His voice sounded like chocolate brandy ought to taste. In a suit whispering Savile Row, and a linen shirt two shades darker than the trousers, he was the epitome of European elegance.

So why did she sense such a dark cloud hovering inside him? He seemed the consummate beautiful stranger. Yet, looking just beneath the surface, she felt not the hunter but the wounded wolf, pushing ancient scars out of existence by force of sheer will. 'Are all your needs being met? Is there anything you need?'

That's not why you came.

Her years of psychology training and practice had kicked in at first sight of him, without consciously trying. The owners of resorts did not commonly knock on doors to check on service levels; that was left to the managers. The resort owners she'd met might come to visit her if they discovered who she was, but they wouldn't have the haunted look of Armand Bollinger's eyes. Beneath the exquisite manners he wore with the same comfort as his excellent clothing, whatever it was he'd come to say sat ill on him.

He knows who I am.

The thought panicked her—but she would *not* show any weakness. She would never give in to any man's demands again.

'Every need has been met, Herr Bollinger, thank you.' She lifted her chin, kept her eyes fully on his. 'Have you come to ask me to leave?'

Armand stared at the diminutive woman before him, her warm curves encased in jeans, a fluffy pink pullover and hotel slippers. Very different from the tiny angles, designer outfits and high heels he'd seen when she was TV's Mrs Dr Pete, the Texan sweetheart who'd made Dr Pete's show the hit it was—or the hit it had been until he'd tossed her off the show. He'd heard it had been canned in the past few weeks.

He'd always been told the camera added ten pounds. It seemed real life did that to Rachel Rinaldi. In fact, if he hadn't seen those fawn-like brown eyes, or her famous smile dazzling his staff through the *terrasse* windows, or heard her pretty, sing-song southern accent telling her story, he wouldn't have recognised her at all. Gone were her trademark mahogany waist-length locks, the flawless make-up, the four-inch heels and the jewellery. In their place were a light-brown pixie haircut and clear, creamy skin with a light dusting of freckles…not to mention the bristling stance and the challenging flash in her eyes as she squared up to him. She was expecting him to throw her out, but she'd go down swinging. But surely she knew why he was here?

She hadn't played the fame card yet to get what she wanted, or to railroad him with their respective positions. *But she will*, he thought cynically. Sooner or later they all did, which was part of the reason he'd left that world years ago. The world his parents had once dominated; oh yes, the Bollingers had been 'beautiful people'.

Then their world had fallen apart, and no one knew it but them. Even now, no one knew the truth of his father's death, or the things he'd done, the family shame.

'If you're going to ask me to leave, Herr Bollinger, I'd appreciate it if you'd get it over with rather than stringing it out this way.'

The aggressive tone seemed off-kilter in her pretty southern accent. Armand didn't start at the somewhat acid return to the present; even his mental shake was unseen. *Give nothing away, don't hand your power to anyone.* He'd learned that lesson long before he'd been kicked out of home at the age of twelve and he'd never forget it.

'You are a paying guest, Ms Chase,' he replied with all the practised smoothness of years, the acting training from young childhood. His father had called them 'deportment classes', but Armand knew them for what they were. *Put on a show, look pretty, display perfect behaviour at all times. No anger, no sorrow, no remorse. And don't ever be yourself.* So he'd play the game she'd set up and see where it led. 'We have just met. Why should you think I wish you to go?'

'Well, you're furious at me for some reason,' she returned, notably less hostile, but with her famed perception.

This time it was harder not to physically react. Damn it, she *knew* what he wanted! Surely she'd known he'd come the moment he found out where she was hiding out? 'Another assumption, given that I've only asked if you need anything,' he said softly.

'You're lying.' With an almost triumphant expression, she pointed at his eyes. 'See, there it is again. It's like lightning behind clouds, the look of fury hiding behind good manners. You're mad at me for some reason, so why not just say so? The sooner you get it off your chest, the sooner I can get back to my lunch.'

Dissected and dismissed within three sentences. Armand wasn't used to either happening to him. Rudeness from guests he could tolerate; stupidity he could ignore, certainly, though it irritated him. The superciliousness and constant demands of the super-rich were every-day life to him, his bread and butter. He'd been unfailingly polite, the perfect gentleman in all the years he'd spent rebuilding the resort and his reputation. The Wolf led the pack. Nobody got the best of him; nobody got *to* him.

How could this total stranger hop the barriers he'd erected twenty years ago with such ease? Damn it, she was laughing at him. Nobody had seen through him since he'd been sent to boarding school at the age of twelve. The day after he'd broken his father's nose.

The night his fairy-tale world had risen up to the light, exposed for the ugly lie it was. The night his sisters had lost their innocence. The night they'd all lost each other. Though they'd gained some closeness since his father had died, somehow it was never the same again.

He caught himself rubbing his finger.

Shut down, turn off. He forced a smile. He was damned if he wouldn't turn the tables. 'All right, then, Ms Chase—or should I say, Mrs Rinaldi?'

Not a muscle moved in her face, but something flickered in her eyes—a fleeting expression he'd seen on a woman's face before, and never wanted to see again. But she spoke calmly, almost bored. 'I realised you'd recognised me the moment you broke into my cabin and heard me speak, Herr Bollinger. Would you mind getting to the point of your visit? My lettuce is wilting as we speak.'

His moment of perception fled beneath the sheer gall of the woman. Now he was less important than lettuce. If Rachel Rinaldi was famed for her loving empathy with strangers, he surely wasn't seeing a sign of it. But, by God, he wouldn't let her get to him—or, more accurately, *keep* getting to him. 'By all means, Ms Chase, return to your lunch. It seems that you need it. Would you mind if I join you?'

The hesitation was so long it was almost as visible as the look in her eyes. She didn't want him here. Never once in his life had a woman refused his company, or even hesitated; always it had been women inviting him, women watching *him* hesitate. Women always had to watch as he walked through his invisible exit sign and never looked back.

He shrugged off the momentary irritation and waited for her to speak. What did he care? This woman was far from his type, and he wasn't looking. He had more than enough to fill his life without coping with a weak, tearful woman's sensitivity, or the ego-filled demands of self-proclaimed strong women hitting him like an axe to the head.

That was the way it always went. His last relationship—if it could be called that—had put him off for a long time to come. Behind her dark, sinuous beauty, Selina had used tantrums, tears, other men and sexual manipulation, all aimed at one thing: to gain the fame of being the woman to tame the Wolf and wear his ring. She'd nearly scratched his eyes out when he'd said only one thing to her as he'd packed his things: 'I don't do cheating women.'

'Certainly, Herr Bollinger,' Rachel Chase said after what seemed an inordinately long time. 'I'm getting a crick in my neck from looking up at you, anyway. Do come in.'

'Thank you,' he said, holding onto his courtesy, seething beneath. This woman wanted him to leave. She didn't feel his famed charm, and his manners only seemed to bring out an irritated acerbity in her he'd never seen on TV.

He didn't care—of course he didn't—but he couldn't help asking himself *why*.

Thrusting the thought away, he called the chef and asked for his lunch to be delivered to the cabin. He held out the dining chair in front of the salad Nicoise which was, indeed, wilting. Once he'd seated her, he called the chef again and ordered a new one despite her protests that it was fine to eat. She sighed and waved a hand around, vaguely indicating all five of the other chairs at the table, as if she didn't care where he sat. 'Please sit, Herr Bollinger.' Inviting him to sit at his own table; he felt the cold fury rack up a notch.

He took the plate of salad away, placing it on

the kitchen counter before returning to her, deliberately sitting opposite her. 'The salad was substandard, Ms Chase. Of course I must replace it with a fresh one. We never serve stale salad in the restaurants, or in the actual hotel rooms.'

'Well, since it was…' And her sentence trailed off. She stared at him, her brow furrowed. 'What do you mean by "actual hotel rooms"? Isn't this cabin reserved for guests?'

He frowned. 'I assumed my manager would have told you—this cabin is only for my private guests, as it's my home.'

If there was one thing he hadn't counted would discompose her, it was that. But there was no way she could fake a face pale to the point of whiteness. No way to darken those big, wistful eyes until they were pure black, pupils dilated with unadulterated fear and horror. 'Oh… Oh, no, no. I didn't… Um, I—I'm so sorry!' she stammered.

No, she couldn't be that good an actress. 'You mean Max didn't tell you when you asked to move in here?' he asked, feeling the inadequacy of the words.

Now it was panic flaring in those easy-to-read eyes. 'I—I must have forgotten. It wasn't Max's fault! He would have told me, certainly. I—I bullied him into it.'

She was babbling. Armand's eyes narrowed as he kept his gaze fixed on her. He'd often found waiting an effective way to make women talk.

She was waiting in her turn, but not to unsettle him. She watched him with the air of one awaiting the guillotine. After a long pause, she whispered, 'Please don't blame your staff, Herr Bollinger. It—it was my fault. I saw the cabin, and—and I wanted more privacy, so I...'

'You bullied Max into it. I see,' he said, trying not to laugh. Half an hour ago, he might have believed it, but now he could no more see her bullying anyone than he could see her drowning a kitten. He didn't have a psychology degree, but his profession required an ability to read people, and something disturbed him about Rachel Chase-Rinaldi.

'And are you aware that other guests are complaining of neglect while at least three members of my staff come here at a time to be regaled with your amusing tales of the life and times of a Hollywood wife?'

Now she looked like a hunted deer, trapped in

the headlights of his interrogation. She licked her lips; her eyes darted around the room, obviously finding no ready answer. At least ten seconds too late, she said, 'It was me, all me. I've…been lonely and, um, they've been doing what your brochure says—taking excellent care of me.'

Every word came out with the fumbling of an honest woman trying to find an excuse. She couldn't meet his eyes as she had so easily while she'd been fighting only for herself.

This was not the woman on the TV who always had the right words to hand, who always knew how to comfort others. So which of the two was the real woman and which was the fake?

'I'll have to commend them, then—but the arrangements will have to change, Ms Chase,' he said quietly. 'The current situation is unacceptable to me, and to my guests and, now I'm here, it will draw the kind of attention I think you wish least.'

The chair opposite him scraped back hard. She got to her feet, sickly pale but with determination in those speaking eyes. 'Of course, I understand. I'll leave on the first train. Do you know if there's one leaving tonight?'

Armand had to fight the urge to blink. Nothing had happened the way he'd thought it would. There was no triumph in running off a woman who looked like a shot fawn.

'You don't need to leave, Ms Chase. If we move you into a suite late tonight, when no one will see, the woman here disappears and you return to being just another guest.'

She shook her head. 'I think it's best if I just go. I've caused enough trouble for you and your people.'

He'd never know later what changed his mind, unless it was the hunted look on her face, the fear she was trying to hide beneath defiance and determination: a sham of strength beneath her pride. The wall surrounding her was crumbling, and she was falling apart behind it. *I have nowhere to go,* her eyes said. Just as his mother had looked the day his father had sent Armand to boarding school. Just as she'd looked the night before he'd left, as she'd watched him taking the blows for her.

'You don't need to leave, Ms Chase,' he said abruptly, wondering what the hell he was saying even as he spoke. 'I have a proposition for you.'

CHAPTER TWO

RACHEL'S jaw dropped. '*What* did you just say?' she demanded when she found her voice. 'No, you couldn't have meant—it's a language miscommunication, right? I'm sure you didn't mean that to sound like…' *You're babbling.* Abruptly she shut her mouth.

For the first time, Armand Bollinger's eyes gleamed with amusement. 'I should have said a *business* proposition. I beg your pardon for the confusion, Ms Chase.'

Though the words were smoothly said, his tone was filled with mirth. He was laughing at her for even thinking he could be attracted to her.

She felt her cheeks heat. 'No, I'm sorry I thought that you could… I realise I'm not…' Once more she broke off. The turbulent confusion inside her had grown to mammoth proportions in the space of seconds. 'Forget I said it,' she muttered, and closed her mouth.

'The word *proposition* is a *double entendre* in itself,' he said, and ended on that odd note. It felt to her as if he wanted to say more, but thought better of it.

The silences were becoming awkward, but she'd only make a mess of it if she spoke.

A knock sounded, and they both jumped to their feet. 'It's all right, I'm closer.' She ran for the door before he could.

His voice came from behind her as she opened the door. 'There are two trays.' He took the heavier one from one of the two staff members at the door, neither of whom were her usual friends. Rachel took the other tray, and with a brief thanks closed the door. Much as she wanted to have a buffer, she was not asking any of his staff to come in. She'd put them all in enough trouble as it was. Disturbed by something, but not sure by what, she returned to the dining room.

'I ordered a white wine. Will you take some?' he asked in a European way as he poured a glass. Looking up with a smile, he held it out to her.

As she took the glass—she loved a good Chardonnay—it occurred to her what she'd seen behind the waiter holding her tray. 'There were people watching us from the restaurant terrace.'

Herr Bollinger nodded as he sat again. 'Naturally, Ms Chase. My regular visitors have worked out that some VIP must have taken over my cabin in my absence—but I saw no one with a telephoto lens, so I doubt they saw you clearly. The cabin's over three-hundred metres from the main resort.' He began eating, seeming unperturbed. 'And that leads me to my original subject. We have a mutual problem, and we need to work out a solution that works for both of us.'

Rachel tilted her head. 'Why is my presence such a problem for you?'

He looked up. 'I don't bring lovers to my home, Ms Chase,' he said, cool as the snow outside. He didn't elaborate. He didn't need to. The lone wolf didn't want to deal with the complications that arose from this: the expectations from the women he dated. 'I expect it will be worse for you, with your husband publicly claiming your reconciliation. The pictures showing you together are obviously a mock-up, since he's in LA and you're here.'

If there was a question in his words, she wasn't

answering. She picked up her fork and began spearing lettuce and tuna.

'Rebuke accepted, Ms Chase,' he said dryly, 'But you can't just hide from the issue this time. We share this problem. I can't sort it out without some sort of communication.'

'Mutual confidences, you mean?' she retorted. 'No thanks. You decide what you want to do. You own the place.' She popped the food in her mouth before she said too much.

After a little silence, he asked quietly, 'Are you always so impetuous? You don't know me. My solution might not suit you at all.'

'You have almost as much to lose as I do,' she said when she'd swallowed her food. She took a gulp of wine—a crime, really, given that it was true Burgundian Chardonnay. 'We both need this resolved with discretion. It's not as if you're going to ask me to be your mistress.'

'Is that so impossible?' he asked with an elliptical smile that set her nerves on edge.

'Given your anger over keeping this as your private hideaway without your future lovers invading? Yes, of course it is.' She shoved a forkful in her mouth, letting him deal with her insights. She was curious to know if he'd be as sarcastic as Pete when she'd out-talked him.

At least I know he won't hit me. I'm a paying guest, and he wants discretion as much as I do. He can't afford to antagonise me.

And the truth of it gave her the courage to speak her mind. She need not fear this man, and that was so liberating, she wanted to laugh with the joy of it. She barely remembered the last time she hadn't been afraid of someone's disapproval.

'I don't know whether to say *touché* or *en garde*,' he murmured, his voice rich with enjoyment. Was he enjoying this crazy seesaw of a conversation?

It was almost a revelation to her—or a revolution; she wasn't sure. Because she discovered, on thinking about it, that she was enjoying it too.

'Feel free to use either,' she said, waving a hand around, mock sword-fighting. She smiled at him.

It felt like a sock in the stomach, seeing that mega-watt, big-as-her-heart smile tossed his way. Armand stopped in his tracks, abruptly lost in it. She wasn't flirting or trying to make a connection. There was no agenda, no personal gain; she was smiling just because she wanted to. And it was like seeing a blazing blue sky after a long, dull winter. The absolute lift of his spirits started low down and finished with a light, silvery feeling in his head, as if he could fly.

Why her effect on him amazed him so much, he wasn't sure, when he'd met a thousand beautiful women—but he definitely didn't want to explore the issue. 'Can we work out stratagems before we duel?' he asked with deliberate lightness. Any kind of probing sent her into tight-lipped silence. He could think of far better uses for that gorgeously smiling mouth the colour of a pink rose.

'Where's the fun in that?' she mock-complained, her eyes shining like sunlight in dark wine.

Damn it, he had to watch his thoughts or he'd be in trouble. The last thing he'd ever do was start up a flirtation with a guest. It led to a hundred different routes, all marked 'danger'.

'You prefer to wing it?' he asked, a deliberate probe. If nothing else, it would cut her friendliness, make her keep her distance again.

And it did. One shoulder lifted in a careless shrug. 'Too many plans ruin the fun. Believe me, I know.' Her voice was wry, and her smile slipped a little.

Armand didn't bother asking the next question

he was sure she wouldn't answer. Besides, something about this woman lit places inside him that had been dark for too long. Though it scared the living daylights out of him, he had to know if it would work more than once. 'Can we at least finish lunch before we begin our riposte?'

She blinked and chuckled. And that damned smile sent warmth and light into him so bright it hurt, little rainbow prism-shots. 'I'm always braver after a glass.' She lifted the wine glass but drank before he could raise his, make a toast or say anything remotely personal.

Why did so much about this woman seem to catch him out? Right now he only knew one thing: he barely knew her. So if he showed any sign of what she was capable of doing to him with a simple smile she'd bolt on the first train. Damn it, she wasn't his type, so why was his body reacting so strongly?

'This wine is heavenly. May I have more?'

Recalled by her abrupt words, Armand realised she'd caught him staring at her; she was blushing, biting her lip. Had his face shown what he'd been thinking? He poured the wine, drank his off and then refilled. 'The vineyard is eight-hundred years old,' he said to fill the silence. 'The grapevines are almost as old.'

'Amazing… Where I come from, anything a hundred years old is historic.' She gulped the entire glass of wine down so fast Armand doubted it touched the edges before she looked at him with hard-earned resolve. 'Look, can you please say what you came to say? The suspense is putting me off my lunch.'

How did she manage it, putting him in his place and making him want to smile at once, so dramatic over a salad? Not to mention the other parts of him that were breaking into an unwanted 'hallelujah' chorus whenever she looked at him or smiled.

Somehow he couldn't dismiss it as a normal male reaction. Probably because this strange connection felt too intimate for just an hour's acquaintance. With her stubborn courage and her willingness to shoulder her own burdens, Rachel Chase touched him somewhere he hadn't felt before. It wasn't normal for him. Usually when he felt something like this it was simple attraction. He'd ask them to dinner, enjoy hearing about the woman's life, take it further at his leisure if she was willing, become bored in weeks and then give the nice kiss-off.

Rachel wasn't anything like the usual women he was attracted to. Yet he was hurting, remembering, thinking—and, yes, he was enjoying himself, merely sitting here talking to her. Within half an hour she'd made him feel more than he had since he'd been twelve.

It only added piquant spice, knowing Rachel didn't seem aware. No feminine antennae were on at all, looking for a man to fill the blank time in her life. She didn't want him at all, barely thought of him as a man.

Then there was the flash he'd seen in her eyes, unmistakable, almost horrifying. For a single moment she'd been afraid of him; she'd been willing to run rather than be near him.

He had to tread lightly here. Just by crossing his own threshold he'd been dragged into undercurrents he wasn't prepared to swim.

'As I said, I know you're Mrs Pete,' he said. 'Given what the media's printed about your personal life, your need for privacy at this time is perfectly understandable.'

One by one, Rachel's vertebrae relaxed. It seemed she wouldn't have to find a new place to go—at least, not yet. 'Thank you,' she said quietly.

'But I need to make some amendments to the current arrangements.' His voice was smooth and even but she almost heard his heartbeat picking up, felt that unknown but strong emotion vibrating through him. 'I have assigned Monika to make up your room and bring your meals while you stay with us.'

Rachel felt the blush stain her cheeks. 'Have there been many complaints against the staff spending time with me?'

Armand Bollinger nodded curtly, and she knew they'd reached the heart of his problem. From what she'd read of him on the plane coming over to Europe, he had rebuilt this place from the ground up after a fire had destroyed almost everything about eighteen years ago—the same fire that had taken the life of his father. The enormous amount of high-flying Guillaume Bollinger's debt only became clear after his death, and speculation was rife on whether his death had been deliberate. Armand Bollinger had just turned seventeen at the time, but he'd taken control of his family finances. With years of hard work and dedication, he'd paid his father's debts before he recreated this five-star resort. He obviously didn't take his success for granted.

Thanks to her, his professional prestige had taken a hit. She knew too well how that felt.

'This situation is my fault.' She gazed at him in determined apology, trying to ignore that odd thrill racing through her body, just by looking into those dark-lashed, storm-grey eyes. An article from about a decade ago floated into her memory: the hypnotic eyes of the Wolf… 'Please don't fire anyone, Herr Bollinger. It wasn't their fault. It was mine.'

'I have no need or desire to fire anyone, Ms Chase. All my staff have given me complete satisfaction until now. I believe everyone deserves a second chance.'

'Oh, yes,' she agreed fervently, though he'd spoken in a voice almost as cold as the snow outside. 'They do. And it really was my fault.'

'So you've now said three times.' As slow as the nod he'd given her moments before, a smile was born. Not the perfunctory stretching of lips she'd seen on rare pictures of him during the past decade, but a real, warm smile. The silly little thrill became outright shivers racing through her as fast as a Daytona driver. She'd seen loads of pretty boys in LA: models, actors and the rest. But she'd never seen such true, strong masculine beauty close up before. When he smiled, Armand Bollinger was *devastating*.

'Moreover, I understand their fascination.' Either not noticing her reaction, or not caring, he lifted the painted china coffee-pot sitting on a matching stand with a candle to keep it warm and offered it to her. Trying her best not to stare at him, she nodded and he poured it into her cup. 'Having a real Hollywood star hiding out in our quiet resort is a scandal too delicious not to take part in.' He held out the coffee cup to her.

She stiffened. 'I thought you of all people would know the truth, Herr Bollinger, given your brief stint as both a French and international *noir* actor, years ago though it was. Stars belong in the sky.' She took the cup and put it down fast; her hands were trembling. 'But I agree that the whole world knows about my life.'

'Or think they do,' he said with a wryness that seemed to come from the heart. 'But, as you know nothing about my real life, I know nothing of yours, Ms Chase. I merely made a generalisation on how average people feel about meeting the rich and famous.'

Startled, she looked up, but his concentration was on his refilled coffee, watching the steam rise. She opened her mouth and then shut it hard. Something about Armand Bollinger was dangerous… and seductive. Oh, he was good, if he could make her yearn to unburden herself within an hour of meeting.

'I guess nobody knows anyone's true story but those involved, unless their publicist gives a quote,' she said lightly. 'But you know the first rule of the media: never let truth get in the way of good sales for the tabloids.' From staring at the curls of steam from her coffee, she looked up with a smile that was its own barrier, daring him to ask.

'So I've heard.' His tone sounded half a million miles away, a lifetime ago.

She found herself staring at him again against her will and even her need. It was as if he'd put her under hypnosis. He had a knack of being able to say so much with a few words, leaving her with the feeling of things unfinished, wanting more. It was as if an asteroid was flying by her, dragging her into its orbit as it passed.

This was the last thing she needed. All she'd wanted was her privacy, to pay her bills when she'd found the strength to face her life. He'd been the one to barge in here, expose her and then say everything and nothing at once. And she *still* didn't know why he was here.

'I think I've asked enough times, Herr Bollinger.' She put down her cutlery and pushed the rest of the salad away from her. More trembling little thrills, more resolute denial. She said calmly enough, 'What is it you're asking of me?'

CHAPTER THREE

AFTER a long moment Armand leaned forward, looking into her face. Those eyes had a power he couldn't define—unless it lay in their utter guilelessness. He'd played the game of love so long with other players, being straightforward with a strange woman felt almost unfamiliar. He followed her suit, pushing his half-eaten lunch away. This discussion was too important to blur with food. 'It's obvious that the past few months have been harder on you than most people know.'

He waited for an answer but, as if refusing to hand her power over even in confirmation or denial, she kept her chin high and said nothing but merely waited.

When it was obvious she wasn't going to answer his unspoken question, to make his task any easier, he decided to plunge ahead. 'You need a place to stay with discreet staff, without needing to go out in public, or do your own shopping, et cetera. My resort is the right place for you. We offer you all the services you need.'

After what seemed like minutes of waiting, she bowed her head, stiff and cold. Just as he'd have done—in fact it was what he had done when he'd been barely seventeen, a rising star in the art-house industry and the secrets surrounding his father's death had been resurrected in the name of public entertainment. 'Go on.'

'But this cabin is my home. If I don't stay in it while I'm here, it will cause the kind of remark and speculation you need least at the moment—but, again, if anyone sees you here and recognises you, you end up with the same problem.'

He saw the flash of fear cross her face before it disappeared. There was something deeper here she was worried about than just her public reputation. 'I don't know whether I caused your problem, you caused mine, or both,' she said, with a slow kind of horror.

'Both,' he replied dryly. 'Mine is but a minor nuisance, Ms Chase. I believe your problem to be more serious.' He left the air filled with the question unspoken. The women he'd known usually rushed to fill a conversational gap if he made it intriguing enough.

This woman didn't even look up, or seem to notice he'd left a half-question dangling there. 'But I caused it. If I hadn't left my room…' Frowning hard, she shook her head.

If he was reading the look in her half-fallen eyes correctly, she felt as guilty as she did fearful—and he had her right where he wanted her. The future of his resorts could be smooth, and her life set back on the right course, with just a little manipulation.

But he'd been hurt and manipulated when he was a boy. Long ago, he'd sworn he would never inflict his will on another, no matter what benefits it could bring him. Yet here he was, playing the worst kind of game, being his father's son. Was history repeating itself—the one thing he'd believed would never happen?

He refused to give in to the guilt coursing through him. *Damn it, this time it's right.*

'All the regular guests will wonder if I don't stay here,' he said, drowning the guilt beneath the weight of arguments he thought would convince her. Yes, he wanted something from her, but he was giving as much as he got, relatively speaking. He might gain financial rewards, but she got what she seemed to need desperately—peace and quiet. 'Apart from family, I've never had any woman here so your presence has already caused speculation.'

Another look crossed her face, similar to when she'd asked about the complaints against the staff. 'I didn't realise…' Her eyes squeezed shut. Her mouth opened, made soundless motions, and then she said faintly, 'Again, I can only apologise for the trouble I've caused you.'

Her embarrassment was too genuine to deny. Armand felt a crazy urge to run out of the cabin, get some fresh air to clear his head. The spoiled-brat media darling he'd assumed her to be an hour ago might have railroaded his staff into bowing to her will, but this woman's conscience seemed even more radiant than her smile. She reminded him of a clawless kitten. Whatever the truth was inside Dr Pete's press releases, a Delilah this woman definitely was not.

This could be almost too easy, except that Armand refused to stoop to stealing candy from babies. Or use another person's conscience against them, to make them sing his tune.

'Since you've made the name change, and with the subtle amendments you've made to your appearance, you could probably take another room without issue,' he said, giving her a last get-out if she wanted to take it. A sap to his conscience, even if he was sure she wouldn't.

'Your staff recognised me within a day, looking just like this,' she replied, with a despairing rather than pugnacious note. 'Apparently, my accent and voice give me away. I've been trying to learn Swiss German, but I'm about as good with accents as I am on skis.'

Armand felt an unusual urge to grin. Rachel Chase seemed almost disastrously honest—a definite downer for hiding in this electronic-media world, but it was a trait he strongly respected. 'Then we go with my plan. I'll stay here with you. I'll go about my business through the day as usual. Monika will—'

'You want me to stay here with you?'

The squeak in her voice wasn't feigned. For all the stories Dr Pete had put out about her, she didn't seem the kind to fall into the arms of a rich man when he showed up on her doorstep—even if it was his doorstep. 'In another bedroom, Ms Chase,' he said in cool amusement. 'The cabin has four of them. You obviously took the word "proposition" to heart.'

A flare of pink touched her cheeks, but her eyes flashed. Though he waited a full minute, she made no retort, didn't try to defend herself. 'Go on,' she said eventually, sounding as angry as she looked.

'It's a necessary evil,' he said, fighting the renewed guilt of knowing he'd backed her into a corner, but torn between anger and amusement at the fact that he'd finally found a woman who not only didn't leap at the idea of staying with him, but fought it all the way. 'My staff's coming and going to the cabin throughout the day while I was gone has already caused curiosity. My regular guests have asked who the VIP is that's staying in my cabin, since I only arrived this morning.'

Again, he saw the riotous flush fill her cheeks. She looked quite pretty like that, in a country-girl fashion. Natural and pure. 'You seem to have learned a lot in a few hours. What did you do, take a general survey?'

She was quick-minded, he'd give her that. 'It's

my job to know what's going on in my resort, Ms Chase.'

'You do it well,' she muttered, but it wasn't a compliment.

He didn't thank her; it would only inflame her anger at suddenly finding herself helpless in a situation that had felt safe until he'd invaded her sanctuary an hour ago. 'As you do your job well, from what I've seen.'

She only shrugged in reply.

Goaded, he said in a silky-smooth voice, 'I asked nothing of my guests, nor did I say anything. I didn't need to. Your total avoidance of the other guests has caused curiosity amongst those who come here hoping for a certain kind of company. My staff has been avoiding all the guests' questions, but you don't want them putting the pieces of your puzzle together. In other words, you need a good cover story, Ms Chase.'

She sighed and nodded. 'Call me Rachel,' was all she said.

'Rachel, then.' In saying her name, Armand took a step into unknown territory. It didn't feel as casual as it had in the past, probably because she'd offered the intimacy with such reluctance. 'I am Armand.'

She only nodded, frowning, serious.

'The assumption is that you must be famous or someone special to me, since my cabin's always been off-limits. The first causes the kind of speculation you need least and, as to the second, my sisters are well known here. I could pass you off as a cousin, but it gives you no reason why you wouldn't mingle with the guests. So either you leave on that train tonight, or become my lover in the eyes of anyone who asks when I refuse to explain who you are.'

He stopped when he saw her pale, a reaction no person could fake. With those enormous eyes, she looked like Bambi after his mother had been shot. 'I think it's best if I leave,' she said quietly, rubbing her wrist with an absent yet anxious movement which was horribly familiar.

Armand's gaze narrowed. He used to do that with his finger in the years before his father had died and he took control of his life.

He went on as if he'd seen nothing. 'But if it got about that you needed to run from here, it would ruin the reputation of my resort—and it has too many potential hazards for you.'

'Such as?' In her clear-to-read expression, there was a mixture of wariness to trust and an almost desperate hope that he had an answer to her problem.

'People already know you're in the run, Rachel— your pictures are on magazines every week. The accent, not to mention the eyes and smile, will give you away. If you leave now and go elsewhere, someone will recognise you, no matter what name you use,' he said quietly.

She let out a tiny sigh. 'That's what I'm afraid of. I thought of using coloured contact-lenses, but over brown eyes it never really works. They end up looking muddy or weird.'

'Disguises aren't the answer. You need to stay out of the public eye for now.' He made the assumption a matter of fact and, as she nodded, he felt the anticipation soaring. 'You're safe here, Rachel.'

The frozen look on her face relaxed. Slowly, the dazzling smile that was as endearing as it was puzzling was turned his way. 'In the time I've been here, every member of your staff has worked hard to protect my identity.'

That smile, not to mention the fear crouching beneath it, left Armand more confused by the moment; all his assumptions had been torn away. From the moment he'd seen her start at the sound of his voice, the fear in her eyes too genuine to deny, the pieces had fallen apart. The rubbing of her wrist left Armand to re-form a puzzle he didn't want to put back together. More than most people, he knew that fame and wealth did not guarantee a happy, trouble-free life.

Rachel wasn't hiding in his resort just to build suspense to the right pitch before granting an exclusive interview to some glossy magazine for the requisite six or seven figures.

'Your need for privacy exactly tallies with my own wishes. I'm about to purchase land for my third resort. Like my first one, it's on the French side of the Swiss Alps. The local authorities investigate all new building projects thoroughly; complaints from my current guests are the last thing I need until the deal goes through. So, by solving both our problems this way, the work on my new resort will go ahead smoothly—if you'll agree to my deal.'

He'd hoped to have her hooked by this time, but she half-tilted her head away from him, her gaze riveted to something about four inches from his face. 'I'm listening,' was all she said, but with the air of waiting for the axe to fall on her.

He leaned forward, hands on the table. 'I stay here as usual, and will order a whole range of groceries to be delivered here, whatever you need. That won't cause remark, as I often cook for myself. Some lunches and dinners I will spend in the resort with the guests, but I'll be here the rest of the time. That's my normal routine and we don't need to break it. If by any chance someone sees you or us together, it's easy for me to pretend to be indulging in a private romance with a mystery woman. Your name will never be mentioned. I'll deal with inquisitive people.' He lifted his brow with a cool, imperious air.

She bit her lip over that stunning, alive smile that filled her face. It made her look like a naughty conspirator. 'I can see how that would work. I certainly wouldn't ask, if you looked at me like that.'

He held in the grin; her mercurial moods were as infectious as they were baffling. 'No member of the press can come unannounced through the gates onto the resort land, since the resort is solidly booked for months in advance. The only way in is through the dated key-card we send guests, and everyone that comes here wants the same level of privacy you need. If you stay here, you'll have the luxury of being able to say nothing. If you cover yourself when you go out, and don't talk to anyone but my staff, there is no reason that anyone should recognise you.'

'You did,' she pointed out. 'Your staff did.'

He gave her a wry smile. 'I heard your voice before I saw your face. It's the voice that gives you away. Your show is on several channels here, dubbed into Italian, French or German for three of them, but the English cable-channel uses your face and voice for an advertisement for the show.'

She frowned and sighed. 'I thought I'd be anonymous here.'

'You are what you are, Rachel, but only for as long as you choose to stay famous. If you want to walk away from the life, people begin to forget soon enough and you can get on with whatever it is you want to do with your future.'

He'd spoken almost harshly, yet she smiled at him as if he'd handed her the key to the door of freedom. 'Thank you,' she said very softly, her eyes alight with relief, her entire face wreathed in the brilliance of her smile.

He had to wrench his gaze from her. When she came alive like that, it almost hurt him to look. 'We can keep the pretence up for as long as you need.'

'Oh, Armand… You don't know what you just said, do you?'

Jerked back by her first use of his name, by the wonder in her tone, he saw the whole room had come alight with the force of that marvellous smile. It was so bright he fought the urge to blink and turn away. 'What?' he asked, fighting to keep his tone even and smooth. For years, he'd kept the façade seamless. How did she pull apart the edges of his control like that and look inside his soul without trying?

'I might want a year, two years—and then you'd be stuck with me,' she quipped, but wryly, so self-mockingly, he wondered if she had any plans to return to her public life. He noticed that she'd neatly sidestepped his subtle query on how much time she'd need with the lame joke.

His brows lifted. 'I doubt it,' he said, just as dryly. 'There's just one personal question I must ask: is there a prospective Mr Chase on the horizon to upset our plans?'

That subtle stiffening of her shoulders spread across her face and body. With deliberate grace, she sipped at coffee that must be nearly cold by now. 'No.'

Though there was an invisible sign screaming 'back off' in neon letters, he forged on. 'And there's no chance of your reconciling with Dr Pete?'

She stilled for a few ticks of the clock, a few moments that seemed for ever. Her fingers rubbed absently at her right wrist again. It was an unconscious movement, a picture that told a million words he didn't want to read. It was almost a full minute before she spoke. 'No.'

Again, it was all she said. Though he waited another full minute for her to continue, she merely lifted her brows and turned her face to the big French cross-beamed doors leading to the balcony. She stared out over the *terrasse* to the Alpine peaks soaring above them with so much absent absorption, it bordered on rudeness.

In Armand's experience, the less he said, the more a woman rushed to fill the silence. But Rachel sat silently, with a half-defiant smile that told him she didn't care what he thought. No details given, not even an explanation as to why there was emphatically no man to fill the void Dr Pete had left.

When she remained stubbornly silent, he tossed a bomb to make her speak. 'Don't you want to know what I wish in return?'

Without looking at him, she said without expression, 'You've already told me, I think. You want me to endorse the new resort for you, to extol the privacy and luxury of this one too, perhaps. You want me to bring other celebrities to your new resort when it's built. You want me to advertise your resorts.'

By now he wasn't taken aback by her perceptive guess—but he noticed that she didn't even ask if she was right. 'Yes, that is what I want,' he said with a similar lack of animation, hiding how damned important it was to him. Someone as loved around the world as Rachel Rinaldi could help him crack the lucrative upper-end of the American market, and she'd fallen right into his lap. He could make the deal without months of negotiations and the endless hassle of speaking through lawyers and agents. He studied her face for a reaction. 'Is it a deal?'

She shrugged with that slow elegance that felt like a wall being erected brick by brick. 'I'm willing to do it, if you're satisfied with such a poor bargain.'

He almost laughed in her face. Getting a woman as world-renowned as Mrs Pete to endorse his resorts was a coup of marvellous proportions for him, and she had to know it. 'A poor bargain?' he asked, tilting his head in clear enquiry. 'Come on, Ms Chase, stop fishing for compliments. The whole world knows you were the one who caused the ratings jump in your husband's show when it began failing. I've heard about the offer made to you since your split with Dr Pete. Your fans demanded you have your own chat show, taking Dr Pete's place.'

'That's no surprise. Thanks to my, eh, husband's

public announcements about his love life and mine, half the world has heard about the offer.'

'It's all over the Internet and the news. People want to know where you are, what you're up to.'

'Trending now,' she retorted in a self-mocking tone. She turned to him at last, but those big eyes were filled with an odd blend of self-deprecating humour and challenge. 'But did you see that I'd accepted the offer? Is your *idea* contingent on my signing up for the show? You may be destined for disappointment.'

'I wasn't thinking of having my resort endorsed by a has-been, despite being one of the ilk myself,' he said curtly.

'I doubt anyone would call you a *has-been*. From what I hear, you chose to walk away from acting at the peak of your career—and this resort is truly beautiful without being overly opulent or flashy.'

He said, touched by the genuine praise, 'Thank you, Rachel.'

She made a thoughtful face. 'You know, when you think about it, loads of products get excellent endorsement returns from the average has-been.' When he least expected it, she grinned. 'I guess the regular Joe on the street will be able to identify with someone like me. My work has always been among the normal people. You're quite perceptive, Herr Bollinger. It may turn out to be a sound business plan, if only your average schmuck could afford to stay here.'

She'd given away more than she knew. 'So Dr Pete lied about the reconciliation and leaving you for the other woman in the first place? You're not taking the job, either?'

Her cheerful demeanour vanished in an instant. 'No comment.'

He squared his shoulders and sat back, only then realising he'd leaned forward, his hand almost touching hers across the table. What the hell had he been thinking to ask? He'd always prided himself on his discretion. So why had he asked?

Because, until now, women have told me their life story without my needing to make an effort. Rachel is my first failure since I was a teenager.

In an attempt to lighten the suddenly charged atmosphere, he said, 'By the way, this is not the place to say "schmuck" to mean a person. People won't understand. The original word means jewellery, mostly used, but it's a general term.'

Her brows lifted, her darkness vanished in an

instant. 'My, how words change meaning in other languages!' And she laughed, a rippling sound, loud and free. When she laughed, Rachel Chase laughed from the heart, and it made him want to laugh with her.

She was a constant surprise to him. Learning the little he knew about her had felt like he'd been pulling teeth, yet it left him feeling oddly fascinated, with a desire to know more.

Rachel was far from his usual type of woman. There was a sense that she'd left the most delicious parts of her conversation unspoken. Perhaps that was the source of his interest? 'Maybe the meaning is not so different,' he suggested, to discover what she'd say. Learning a single fact about this woman took more digging than he'd ever needed before. 'It's still something used, something tossed aside because someone no longer wanted it.'

She pulled a thoughtful face, looking like a pensive pixie. 'That makes sense. We Americans merely made the leap from thing to person. Poor schmuck,' she said again, and laughed. As if the sun had come out from behind clouds, the room seemed to light up with her face.

Armand had to drag his gaze away and get back

to the business at hand. 'So are you agreeable to my idea? If so, I'll bring my suitcase in. Which bedroom are you using?'

She pointed to a door.

'Ah, my mother's old room.' Before she could do more than briefly look horrified, he put up a hand. 'Maman lives in her own house a few hours' flight from here. She visits a few times a year. She's not coming until summer now. She would be the first to say you're welcome, Rachel.' The name kept slipping so naturally from his lips, he barely noticed. 'I'll keep my room. The third is now a study, if you've noticed, with wireless Internet and computer. I can work in the hotel for a few hours a day, and if you need to work—' he saw her stiffen again and added '—or need to keep up your communications, feel free.'

'Thank you.' Her voice was subdued, but she neither confirmed nor denied the subtle probe. It seemed he'd finally met the woman who didn't want or need to defend herself against the accusations her ex had levelled at her. Whatever the truth was inside the story of Dr and Mrs Pete's break-up, Rachel Chase obviously did not want or need to unburden herself to a stranger about her life, no matter how much he was helping her.

He didn't care if she wanted to keep to herself—actually, it was quite refreshing. So from now on she would have what she wanted from him: peace and quiet.

'I need to work for a couple of hours. I'll be back before dinner.' He gathered the lunch plates and coffee paraphernalia on one tray and stacked the other beneath. 'There's no point in hiding that I have a guest stying with me when people saw you take the tray. Do you mind if I order dinner for us? Is there anything you don't like? What do you like to drink—wine, water, soft drinks?'

'I don't eat really spicy food, it burns my stomach,' she confessed with a fledgling smile.

Strange, the way her smile hit him every time. Every time she did it, something or someone new seemed to peep out from behind the confident, caring persona of the woman he'd seen on TV—neither the frightened kitten nor the cool, defensive rebel he'd dealt with today. 'And what is your drink of choice?'

'I tend to stick to water at night, though I love the hot chocolate they make here.'

'Consider it done; I'll order both.' He picked up the tray. 'I'll see you later.'

'Um, Herr Bollinger?'

He turned at the door, looking over his shoulder. 'My name is Armand.'

'Armand...' The name rolled off her tongue with that gorgeous southern accent of hers. It sent the oddest feeling through him, a sense of waiting fulfilled. 'Thank you. I'll try not to be too much trouble.'

He almost said *a paying guest is never trouble*, but he held it in. Seeing the smothered anxiety beneath her calm façade, he wondered what had happened to make her feel unworthy of even the most basic help—but he was afraid he already knew.

'I am doing very little,' he said coolly. 'A few weeks sharing my cabin, and I get an endorsement of my resort in return.'

When he saw her shoulders finally relax, he felt the tension disappear from his body, but when he left the cabin his mind was racing. If a woman as loved by her fans as Rachel Rinaldi could feel that she was a bother just by sharing his cabin, there had to be a damned good reason.

There must also be a reason why she wasn't giving her side of the story to the world. Surely she must know that, given her intense popularity, she'd be believed?

There were definite, unexpected depths to this woman, layers she didn't want him to see, things he didn't want to know.

He'd failed *Maman*—he'd left her to the abuse he couldn't stop until his father's death. He didn't know what the hell he could do to help Rachel. Anything he tried would probably make things worse. But he was committed to spending the next few weeks with her.

So what could he do to ensure it wasn't a disaster that would send her running from here before he got his endorsement?

CHAPTER FOUR

'WHAT is this?'

Rachel looked at the electrical apparatus sitting in the centre of the table with vague suspicion. It looked like some sort of grill, with small-handled pots beneath the heating bars. A wonderful smell permeated the air: cheesy, but like no cheese she'd ever eaten. Bowls of food sat around the grill and a range of foods was sizzling on the rectangular grill-plate above.

'You haven't had this before?' Armand asked, looking surprised. 'You've been in Switzerland for weeks. Surely Max recommended it at least once?'

When she shook her head, he smiled with what looked like genuine pleasure. 'Then I shall be the first to share this experience with you. This is *raclette*, a traditional Swiss food for winter—but usually it's only served with potatoes and pickles. I like to switch it up a bit, add more to the menu.'

'It smells divine.'

He used little wooden spade-like objects to flip the food over. 'I order this for my first dinner whenever I return from being away.'

For a moment the impulse to ask where he'd been rose in her throat, but she forced it down. It wasn't as if they were friends. They were strangers sharing a cabin and an agreement, no more. He'd respected her secrets; she would be showing the worst form of ingratitude if she didn't do the same for him.

The trouble was that his patter, and the new food, had begun to relax her from the feeling of trepidation at his return tonight—that, and the jeans and sweatshirt he wore, both old but comfortable, by the looks of it. Everything felt informal, especially Armand himself—as if it was a deliberate ploy. She couldn't help but wonder if there was something else he wanted from her.

But the way he moved in those clothes was so fluid, with such natural grace, she felt a surge of envy—and another emotion she didn't want to identify. But she was a functioning woman, and any woman still breathing had to appreciate a man this masculine and this beautiful.

Although she'd showered this evening, she was still wearing a simple jeans and pullover. It was all she'd brought with her when she'd fled LA. She'd left everything behind: her name, her trademarks, any and all memories of Pete and her TV persona. And every day that she pulled on her comfy clothes, saw her natural brown hair, ring-free left hand, no make-up and didn't have to endure another day of hunger to remain svelte for the camera was another happy day.

There was no way she'd play the perfect doll again. Not for any man.

But her half-hearted attempt at defiance died with her first sight of him in his jeans. Without that little surge of rebellion to protect her emotions, she felt naked. She'd never been happy without having some form of barrier. Her mother had taught her that. Her mother's ladylike behaviour had been her protection from the hurt from her daddy's careless philandering.

But no form of refined protest Rachel tried had ever stopped Pete from railroading her. Nor did it seem to work with Armand. She guessed she just didn't have the way of it.

'Please, come and sit down,' he said with a

smile, as if he hadn't noticed her silence. 'It's ready to eat.'

'Full points to Monika for the setting,' she murmured as she sat down, anxious to give her new friends all the praise she could.

Armand moved her chair in. 'Monika is finished for the day, but I will pass on thanks to the appropriate place.'

'Thanks,' she sighed, reflecting on Armand's courtesy with a slightly uncomfortable feeling. Probably his good manners were ingrained in him, but it had the feel of subtle undercurrents, as seductive as they were dangerous. She felt as if she'd fallen into unfamiliar waters from the moment he'd come into her life, pulling her with gentle insistence out to sea.

Don't think about it. Don't look at him. Frowning, she looked beneath the grill plate and saw cheese bubbling in the little flat pans. 'This looks delicious.'

'It is, and so easy. Just cook what you like to eat, and when it's ready pick what you want to eat, put it on your plate and pour the cheese over.'

The flavour burst on her tongue with the first mouthful. 'Oh, this is superb, Armand,' she murmured when her mouth was empty. 'No wonder it's a national dish—I'd eat it—'

'Rachel?'

Her eyes snapped open at his tone of voice which, though quiet, held inexplicable warning. A tiny shiver ran through her spine and she forgot about the food. 'What is it?'

He was looking only at his plate, seeming to enjoy the smell of his food. 'Someone's watching us through the *terrasse* door. She's looking right at you.'

She heard one of her vertebrae snap into place as she straightened, but she didn't look around. 'You said *she*?'

'Try to relax, Rachel,' he said softly, still not looking at her. 'It's okay. I recognise her. It's Amelia Heffernan, a regular visitor to the resort— she's a widow, an incurable romantic, and also incurably nosy. She only arrived today. She must have heard the rumours of a woman staying here and came to check for herself.'

One by one, her vertebrae relaxed again. She drew in a breath, her first in almost a minute. She looked at him, trying not to show her fear. 'Does she watch TV?'

'She's elderly—of course she does. And, yes, she loves the chat shows.'

Rachel turned cold all over. 'Armand, if she recognises me and tells anyone...'

She couldn't quite interpret his smile. 'From where she's standing, she can't see your face. Stand up and come to me.' He rose to his feet, moving to her. '*Smile* at me. Our ruse won't work if you look like you'd rather walk into an iron maiden than into my arms.'

She looked down, shaking her head. 'I can't do it. I just can't.'

He reached her chair, but didn't touch it, only her shoulder. 'Rachel,' he murmured, 'You don't know me. You have no reason to trust me. But right now I'm all you have.'

Slowly she lifted her face, turning her neck so she looked into his eyes. In them she saw not the predatory male after dominance, not even tenderness, but a reluctant understanding. It made her breath catch.

'Sometimes you have to leap,' he said quietly. 'It's your choice.'

He was right. It had to be now or never.

Her heart beat a hard tattoo as she rose to shaky

feet and he turned her body so she was in his arms. The look on his face was confident, a man sure of his welcome. Suddenly she couldn't breathe…

'It's just like those days when the last thing you wanted was to be in front of the camera, Rachel. Remember? I'm smiling for her. If I must, I'll kiss you for her. But none of it's real. It's all rehearsed. It's not who we are. This man is not who I am. I'm helping you, nothing more.'

Rachel gulped, and nodded. Somehow his words made it easier to snuggle in. 'It's not real,' she whispered to herself as she wrapped her arms around his neck. 'It's not real.'

'This is the only way she won't be able to see your face from any angle,' Armand whispered, holding her against his body, her cheek against his heart.

Despite the tender reassurance, she suddenly rocketed back a few months in time, standing in Pete's arms, waving to the audience the day after he'd first hit her. 'Smile, Rachel,' he'd muttered. 'They all love us. Smile for them.' He'd squeezed her waist, right where he'd hit her the night before after seeing that her fan rating was higher than his.

He had been reminding her of who was in control, both in the show and in life.

'Rachel?'

Her vision cleared, and she saw Armand looking down at her, tender and troubled. He wasn't Pete, and she felt safer with this stranger than she had with anyone in a long time.

That gave her the courage to try. 'Smile at me,' she muttered through gritted teeth. 'She'll never believe it if you look at me like you're scared I might break any second.'

He gave a soft chuckle and lowered his face to hers. Rachel jerked back before she could stop herself. 'Make the leap, Rachel,' he whispered, moving close again. 'Trust me.'

She bit her lip, saw that look again, the sadness and the pain beneath the confident hunter—the wounded wolf. She gave permission in a tiny nod. 'Do it.'

His lips barely touched one side of her mouth, and then the other side, in sweet mimickry of the real thing, leaving her heart banging like a jackhammer right up as high as her throat. Then he drew her closer still but, though it looked loving— seductive even—she was in his arms in a hold more gentle and protective than any she'd ever known. 'I'm not him,' Armand whispered into her hair.

Slowly, still trying to take air into lungs that wouldn't behave and fill, she nodded. Not real? It was all too real, and something buried deep inside her came shimmering back to life. She could hardly remember the last time anyone had held her, unless it was for an audience. Though they had an audience of one now, Armand's tender hold made her feel as if they were alone, that he was holding her because he wanted to…

He bent down to murmur against her ear. 'Frau Heffernan has been coming to the resort since its reopening, and is very loyal. She just wants to know what's going on. So, for now pretend to dance with me. She'll interpret it as a private romance. She'll love having the power of knowledge no one else has and, beyond teasing me about it in quiet moments, nothing will be said, certainly not in public.'

With a tender hand he moved her head so her face was buried against his chest as he hummed a song. He moved her in a slow shuffle, always keeping her face from the clear *terrasse* doors, protecting her with every movement he made.

She felt so safe. She felt his heart beating against her cheek, heard the swishing of his breath in and out as they danced. He wound his fingers through hers, held her waist with a light, reassuring clasp. How he managed to give her personal space when he held her like a lover, she couldn't understand—but he did. Somehow he knew she couldn't bear any form of male dominance.

He'd given her the choice in everything since he'd invaded her life.

It was a revelation to her as new and wondrous to her as a bud unfurling. Armand had walked away from the life Pete craved like a drug. Armand allowed her to hold her power without punishing her for it. And, yes, he let her know who was in control—*she* was.

His arms were so gentle, his hands so tender. She wanted to melt into him, to fall into this safe, beautiful place and never leave…

No. She'd been alone too long, that was all. Even on her wedding day part of her had felt lonely and lost. At nineteen she hadn't known why; at thirty-two, she understood. Though Pete had always been extravagant with compliments and the words 'I love you', his self-love was all-absorbing, and allowed for nothing but the shallowest of affection for anyone else. The day she'd rebelled against his wishes, he'd shown her who was boss in punishing blows.

But now Armand had come into her life with his tender arms and his kindness, and he was a greater threat to her well-being than if he had been holding a sub-machine gun to her head.

And yet she couldn't move from this hold, more seductive than any practiced caress could be. No wonder they called him the Wolf. He knew how to charm her into a state of hypnotic compliance, trusting him within hours of meeting him.

'Is she gone?' she whispered after what seemed like hours, minutes, seconds—she couldn't work it out but, while it seemed too long, it wasn't long enough.

He's a stranger. She needed space now.

'Not yet,' he said quietly. 'She's got her heavy-weather gear on. She's there until we notice her.'

Her fingertips were quivering as she fought against running, against holding on with all the strength she had. 'What do you think?'

'It's your call, Rachel. I can look at her, embarrass her into leaving.'

About to assent, she thought of what it might cost him as the owner and hesitated. 'Would you do that if I were a woman you—you…?'

'Wanted to make love with?' His voice sounded smoky now, and a hot shudder touched her skin with slow, sensuous fingertips. 'No, I probably wouldn't have noticed her at all. By now I'd have carried you to the bedroom.'

Gulp, gulp… The lump in her throat just wouldn't go away. 'I…Herr Bollinger…'

'It's Armand—and if I carry you to the bedroom tonight it will only be for show. I don't abuse women, or persuade them against their will, Rachel Chase. Remember that.'

At that, she stilled so totally she felt her pulse in her throat—and then from somewhere inside her, the fighter came back. 'Then don't speak to me so intimately. We're strangers sharing a cabin, no more than that—and, please remember, I'm still a paying guest.'

'*Touché*, Ms Chase. That's very good.' A rumbling laugh rippled through his body and, though she fought against his power, he still infected her with his mirth. 'And I will *not* point out that the fact that we're in this situation is totally your own fault because you moved in on my private domain. My mother raised me to be a gentleman.'

She grinned against the windcheater he wore, which was as warm as his teasing comment. 'And my mama raised me to be a southern lady. So don't touch me without permission, Armand Bollinger. You might be a wolf, but I can become a she-bear without warning.'

'Consider me appropriately chastened.'

The laughing tone made her feel absurdly happy. 'How weird is this conversation, given our current circumstances?' she whispered, feeling his skin touching hers. They were only hand to hand, cheek to cheek, but it moved with invisible fingertips into her soul.

'That's just what I was thinking.' He relaxed his arms and looked down at her, smiling.

Oh, those silly hot shivers! 'So, is she still there?'

He checked briefly without seeming to. 'She is, in a covered corner of the *terrasse*, and watching us avidly. Time to implement plan B—the wolf must dare the she-bear and we'll see who wins.' He lifted her in his arms, his eyes twinkling as he smiled down at her. Slowly, he rubbed his cheek against hers with absolute gentleness. 'You're a very little bear. I can *bear*ly feel you.'

Warm, safe and beautiful all at once—oh, this man was too seductive for his own good in making her feel this way, even when he was trying to reassure her with his teasing. 'Ha ha. That's because I'm fading away from hunger,' she complained, trying to joke her way into a normal breathing pattern and heartbeat.

He sniffed and his face darkened. 'The cheese is burning.' He put her back down in her chair, turned back and strode over to the *terrasse* doors. After flashing a dark look at the elderly lady, he wound the built-in blinds down. He kept going even after the startled Frau Heffernan had scuttled away. 'Good, now we can eat. I'll clean the pans and be right back.'

Rachel was glad she was sitting down. Her knees really didn't want to be straight at this point.

Armand's knees seemed just fine. After he picked up the collection of little trays, he headed for the kitchen with a clean, confident stride. 'Can you turn the heat down on the grill and take the food off the top while I clean these, please,

Rachel? I'll be back in a few minutes. Hopefully everything won't get too cold.'

He spoke in his ordinary voice, as though nothing had happened.

Perhaps to him it hadn't.

'Okay, consider it done.' After speaking as calmly as possible, Rachel drew a deep, slow breath, wondering how the world could turn upside down in a few hours. From feeling safely hidden away, she was out of her depth in waters as sweet as they were turbulent, and all because of one tycoon in shining armour...

Feeling a fervent kinship with the elderly woman—she wanted to scuttle away from Armand too, never come back and definitely never see him again—she made a noncommittal noise of assent and began moving the food from the grill.

'Don't think about it, just don't think about it,' she chanted beneath her breath. She shoved a crispy piece of bacon on her tongue and chewed on it despite the fact that it tasted like ashes in her mouth.

What just happened in there?
Armand leaned against the sink for a moment,

just breathing. He tossed the *raclette* trays in the sink and ran warm, soapy water over them. Even as he cleaned out the hard cheese and washed them he was conscious of the crazy feeling that had sent him running in here. It hadn't lessened, despite the space between them.

So stupid, to lose his temper over something as simple as burning cheese! He supposed he'd had to do something—and it was either take out his sudden anger on the *raclette* grill and Frau Heffernan, a rich widow without a life of her own, or give in to the consuming need to touch Rachel again.

How idiotic was it to touch a woman in his own home? And yet it felt so right.

He'd never brought a woman here, apart from Maman, Johanna and Carla. It was their home as much as his, since Papa had left it to them all equally. It had been almost all he'd had left to give after the fire destroyed the first resort, and he'd gambled away everything else. To Armand, this cabin was his home, a sacred place of refuge. He'd never brought a woman here until now.

At first, he'd thought it was simple pity. She was

alone in a world turned against her, and her jerk of a husband had betrayed her publicly.

Then he'd seen the way she rubbed at her left wrist almost absently, as if in reminder. Maman had done the same thing, long after the breaks had healed from his father's repeated beatings. When Rachel had caught him looking, she'd tried to hide it far too quickly, just as Maman had.

Armand seethed and burned still, just thinking about the shame and embarrassment on Rachel's face. If that damned 'doc with empathy' had been here right now...

It came down to this: Rachel Chase needed protection from Rinaldi, and he could give it.

And you have to do it, because you didn't protect your own mother.

There was the crux of it. More than twenty years ago, Armand had woken one night to see the truth he'd probably always known—his father had beaten Maman two shades too hard to hide the bruises; he'd broken her arm.

Armand couldn't change the damage done to his family, but he'd stop Rinaldi from damaging Rachel any further. If Rinaldi showed up, he'd be here waiting.

Despite her spunk and her volatile changes, her inner strength and perception, Rachel was no she-bear. She couldn't protect herself physically against the likes of Dr Pete, let alone stand against the media onslaught. Armand had the skills, the wealth and the place to protect her—and the reputation didn't hurt. If Rinaldi showed his face here, he'd meet with the Wolf, all right—a wolf in protective mode. He didn't care what it took right now, he'd keep Rachel safe.

But he could not and would not hold her again. It was too dangerous to the calm demeanour she needed from him. She needed to heal, not have her protector fantasising about making her his lover. And to make sure she was safe, he had to be in control of his emotions.

Damn it, when has touching a woman ever been this emotional for me?

'So stop looking at her. Stop thinking about it,' he growled to himself.

Stop remembering how it felt to hold her.

He had to remember instead that she'd called him Herr Bollinger, putting space between them the moment he'd shown her that his male imagination was running riot. *She's been through enough.*

*She doesn't want you for anything but protection.
She needs a friend.*

So a friend he'd be. Nothing had happened, really—just a new kind of male reaction to a sweet, curvy bundle of woman in his arms. End of story.

But every single one of the cheese trays had grooves in them from the steel wool he'd gouged into them with his cleaning efforts when he carried them back into the dining table.

When he glanced at her, she was sitting in her place with seeming calm, but her fingers were laced so tightly together they had white patches. Looking up, he saw the apprehension in those shimmering, far-too-expressive eyes, and the paleness of her cheeks.

Had he frightened her with his emotions? He smiled in rueful apology, but it felt as if he'd gouged his smile in place too. Reassure her; be gentle. A friend, only a friend.

This was going to be a very long few weeks.

CHAPTER FIVE

IT was almost nine the next morning when Armand—who'd risen at six, had showered, enjoyed breakfast and was currently working from the cabin office—heard the door of the other bedroom squeak slightly as if being opened. 'Good morning, Rachel,' he called.

He received only a grunt in reply. From the open door, he saw a pyjama-clad form holding a bundle of clothes dash past him to the bathroom. The door slammed behind her.

With raised brows, he kept working. Somebody, it seemed, was not a morning person—or, like most women he'd met, Rachel didn't like appearing before others while she was looking her worst.

Not that she did. The brief flash past him had been candy-pink, all tousled hair, rumpled clothes, curvaceousness and, altogether, rather delicious.

Stop it. With a determined growl, he pushed the vision of her from his thoughts and kept working on the latest round of paperwork from the local officials for the new land.

Somebody obviously also liked long showers. It was almost half an hour later when she finally emerged. Her curvy shape was encased in similar jeans to last night, and a long-sleeved T-shirt with 'sometimes your knight in shining armour is just a jerk in tin foil' emblazoned on it. Clear-painted toes peeped from the open-ended hotel slippers. Her hair was shining, cheeks flushed and her skin glowed with health. Again, her face was free of make-up, but she still managed to look radiant. It was her eyes, her smile. With those weapons at her disposal, she'd never need the rest.

'Now I'm human enough to say hi,' she announced gaily as she shuffled towards him, the slippers making a soft swish-swish on the wooden floors. 'Good morning, Armand. Did you sleep well?'

About to ask the same thing, he nodded, surprised anew that 'Mrs Pete' would be the one to ask first. 'Thank you. And you?'

She nodded in return. 'The beds here are very comfortable.'

'You've been here a few weeks now, I believe.

Do you have any thoughts on ways to improve the standard of the resort?'

Her smile slipped a touch. A wary kind of nervousness entered her eyes. He didn't know what was going on. Such an innocuous question shouldn't send her running for cover. 'I only asked because I wish to attract all kinds of international guests.' he said gently. 'I've catered in the European style. You're American—your honest opinion is the kind of feedback I need.'

'Oh.' She relaxed so visibly he could almost see her muscles uncoiling. 'Well, while the rooms are wonderful, for people that want real privacy, or for family vacations or reunions, cabins like this would be in demand, I think.'

He frowned. 'The suites aren't enough?'

'Oh, they're wonderful,' she rushed to say. 'I—I was just thinking—you know, forget it. What do I know? I never stayed at a place like this until I was an adult. Your guests probably don't want kids and noisy families here. It was a stupid thought.'

'Rachel.' With a hand on hers, he stopped the babbling. 'I did cater this first resort for adults, and the second in Chamonix, but I want to extend for the third, make it more family-friendly. I loved it when we stayed here when I was a boy. Providing cabins helps the resort to compete with the sport hotels and bed and breakfasts.' He typed the information quickly into the email he was composing to his architect and sent it. 'Done.'

Then he turned to her and smiled again. 'Thank you for that, Rachel. The more ideas I provide for the third resort, the better chance I have of acquiring the land. Laws for building resorts can be rather stringent here.'

'You're welcome,' was all she said, but the look of shy delight on her face both moved and puzzled him. This level of insecurity surely went deeper than his suspicions. How could a woman so famous for giving good advice not be jaded by people's thanks?

You're getting in too deep here. She isn't Maman. You can't balance your debt to Maman and the girls by helping this woman.

He knew nothing of her outside the tabloids, such as why she had the name 'Rhonda Braithwaite' on her suitcases and 'Rachel Chase' on the passport she'd given at the reception desk. He didn't know if she was a good person or...

Yes, he did know that, by the way she'd shouldered the blame instead of letting a single member of his staff be reprimanded. He knew it by the horror on her face when he had told her this was his cabin. He knew it by the way she hadn't tried to bargain with him over his deal, though she had to know who was getting the better end of it.

And, damn it, he knew how good it felt to hold her in his arms—and he knew she'd felt it too, even if she didn't want to be there.

Whether he wanted to get involved or not, he was already in way over his head here.

'You never answered me yesterday, when I asked how long you thought you'd need my help here.' He kept the question gentle, masking the intense need to show the turbulence inside. His anger wasn't aimed at her, but at the men of the world who felt it was their right to abuse a woman or a child. Anger, because it seemed impossible to change one man's way of thinking and behaviour, let alone the world's. *It will never happen again,* they always said, until they lost their temper again.

'Is time an issue for you? If so, I can go any time, really.'

Armand heard the undoubted tone of fear beneath the projected calm in her voice. She was using every trick in her psychologist's book, not to charm him or pry into his life, but to hide her deepest emotions from him.

'Well, it could be an issue if you were planning on staying here for the next five years,' he said, angling for a laugh, or at least to make her relax a bit. 'I do have three resorts to manage—at least once this next one's built.'

'And you ought to be there to oversee the project.' The words were sympathetic now the psychologist's persona she slipped into without a problem. He thought it was because then she could hide her real self—the woman she was ashamed of being. 'As I said, there's really no issue if you have to go at any time. If you don't mind me staying, I'll be fine here alone.'

Yet it *was* a problem for her. He knew that, but he had no right to ask. Even being her temporary protector didn't cancel out the fact that he'd known her less than twenty-four hours. He couldn't butt in on her private world.

So he tried the one way that seemed to work for her. 'And still she doesn't tell me her time frame. Rachel Chase, international woman of mystery… You didn't tell me you worked for MI6. Or the

CIA, since you're American. Or are you?' he riposted with a grin.

Her face relaxed. She bit her lip, but laughed anyway. She laughed like a child every time, laughed as though she meant it. It lit up the room. It lit up his safe, predictable world, and filled it with warmth, colour and enchantment.

'Is two weeks okay with you, maybe three?'

The words broke into uncomfortable conclusions, giving the rainbow light and myriad warmth a time-limit. He was relieved; of course he was. It was best this way, short and sweet. He'd had small infatuations before with unattainable women and he'd recovered. Yes, he liked Rachel—found her adorable, damn it—and he definitely liked the way she felt in his arms. But it wouldn't be a tragedy if she left tomorrow or the next day. Or in two weeks or three. He was stronger than that, had survived a lot worse disasters than a woman leaving his life after a few weeks. *Facile venir, facile aller*—easy come, easy go—that was his motto.

'Good,' he replied at last, with a cheerfulness that seemed overdone, even to his paranoid ears. 'Two weeks is definitely doable—or even three or four.'

'Really? I can stay? It's not an issue for you?' she asked, her eyes wide and her smile bouncing off those unseen prisms in the room. Rainbow reflections were everywhere...

He felt his eyes blink in astonishment at having made an offer she hadn't asked for. What was wrong with him lately? 'Yes, of course,' he said smoothly. 'You are a paying guest, after all.'

Something came and went in her face, a frisson of apprehension. Her smile faded to something weak and half-hearted. 'Well, then, we both know where we are. The day I run out of funds, I'll be out of your hair for good, Herr Bollinger.'

Brave words, but her fingers trembled. And he could have kicked himself. No doubt Dr Pete had frozen the accounts, hoping that sooner or later his newly renamed wife would be forced to come into the open and use electronic funds to survive. Then he could find her, and bring her to heel. She might already have run out of money.

It was only when she'd left the room, still clutching at her pyjamas—cute pink things with little cats on the telephone—that he realised she hadn't called him Armand since he'd brought up the subject of her stay. She knew he was trying to manipulate her, however subtle he'd been in his effort. He'd tried to dig into her life, and again she'd given nothing away.

Two, maybe three weeks was all he had to get her out of danger—that was, if she didn't run out of funds first. And, given his complete failure in getting a single personal concession from her, three weeks wouldn't be nearly enough.

Without needing to think it through, he emailed Max again.

Nobody is to mention funds to Ms Chase. She is our honoured guest, for as long as she needs to be here.

He said nothing else, but he knew Max wouldn't ask. It was Armand's practise to allow respected clients some space and time to pay their bills. He'd always judged this by instinct alone and he'd never been wrong. They always came through sooner or later, and they'd all become numbered among his most loyal returning guests or even investors.

Now all he needed was to think of a reasonable excuse that would allow her to stay and still satisfy her pride. He just knew that, if he couldn't come up with something really good, she'd leave with her head high, refusing his charity. He couldn't let her vanish without trace, not when he was sure that sooner or later, she'd run into more trouble than she could handle alone.

That afternoon

'It's a simple contract, Rachel. You stay here until I've secured the new resort and I have the architect's plans. Then I'll take you there, and you can endorse at least two of my resorts with honesty.'

Rachel frowned at Armand, sensing something deeper than he was showing with this perfect courtesy. 'Why do you need me to sign a contract? I've said I'll do it.'

His eyes darkened to stormy grey, the hidden lightning beneath the handsome diplomat's face. He only looked like that when he was hiding something. 'Because then, if you change your mind and sign on for that show, or pursue other avenues with your career, you're legally bound to this venture first.'

'I've never broken a contract in my life,' she replied, aiming for calm, but knowing her voice shook a little. 'Whatever you've heard about me...'

His facial muscles didn't shift; he looked calm, but she sensed the tempest buried deep inside his emotions, like black clouds on the edge of a summer-blue sky. 'I've heard nothing to your detriment, Rachel. I don't buy tabloids for entertainment. I'm merely used to conducting my business on more than a handshake or verbal agreement. I've found it's safer that way—for both of us.'

'I see.' Now she couldn't keep the stiffness from her tone. No matter how he couched it, it was obvious that he didn't trust her. 'Then I'll fax a copy to my lawyer and have him read over it before I sign.'

A short pause, then he said, 'Are you certain it's wise to contact someone from home?'

No matter how tactfully he'd said it, the unspoken knowledge hovered between them. Silence had become her bulwark and shield, but with a few tactful words he'd given her a timely reminder. Yes, Pete *would* lean on her lawyer to divulge her whereabouts, should she contact him. She already knew he'd done the same with her parents and her sister, Sara. Until she'd turned off her phone, all their calls had been reproaches about abandoning 'poor Pete' in his time of need.

That Armand hadn't spoken about Pete directly showed she was right. He already knew or suspected far too much.

'Then I'll find a lawyer in Zürich. One that speaks English,' she added defiantly, before he could say it. 'There must be loads of them.'

'There are, and that's your right, certainly. You don't know me, and I don't know you. It's best we keep this entire matter as a business arrangement.' His tone was as withdrawn as hers. Though she knew it was stupid, she wondered what she'd said or done to put distance between them when just last night, they'd been so close.

Don't think about it.

Like it or not, separated or not—even though Pete had cheated on her at least twice—she was still a married woman for another few weeks. She had no right to think about how much Armand's holding her last night had affected her, let alone keep reliving how safe she'd felt How warm and tender his arms and hands had been. And the look in his eyes…

No. She had to remember, this arrangement was all just business: *keep Rachel happy, keep her here, let her think you might be interested until the resort's endorsed. And, if the ads fail, drop her like a hot potato.*

That's why he's called the Wolf, right? He'll do whatever it takes to make his ideas work. It's said he hasn't failed at anything he's taken on since he was seventeen.

And yet, impatient with this wary reserve, sick of trusting no one, she picked up the five-page contract and read it through. It was exactly as he'd said: straightforward, no hidden clauses. She was to stay here free of charge until the deal went through for the resort on the Swiss side of the French border. Then she would appear on a series of endorsements for the Bollinger resorts, and that would be that.

'You're right, it's very simple.' Drawing a fast breath, she grabbed the pen and signed it. 'There you are, Herr Bollinger, it's all done. Now you can get back to work.' Bundling the sheaf of papers in her hands, she shoved it at him as if palming off a grenade. Some instinct was screaming at her, *you'll regret this.*

Expecting further withdrawal on his part, or cold satisfaction at his victory however he won it, she was taken aback by the brief flash she saw in his eyes—it almost looked like relief. And that sent a spurt of confusion and worry through her. He *did* know too much. 'Thank you, *Rachel*.' And, if there was a slight emphasis on her given name, the crispness of his voice and the way he signed the papers, straightened them and put them in a folder was all business. 'I have a meeting with the staff for the rest of the afternoon. I'll be back in time for dinner.'

Rachel watched him leave the cabin, torn between indignation and aching wistfulness: a spurt of loneliness that hurt her heart but had little to do with being alone. She tried to shake it off, but it persisted through a two-hour session of reading, writing in her journal and listening to music. It continued even through an hour-long tramp along one of the marked nature-trails. Sweating through the layers she had to wear for her anonymity hadn't bothered her until today.

But there were three things she didn't and wouldn't do: check email, check her SMS's or watch TV. The first two were easily traceable if Pete paid an expert enough, and watching TV was a reminder of the woman she used to be. The longer she stayed here, the more she wondered if she should ever have been that person at all.

So who was she now, and what did she want from life?

For someone who'd lived her entire life on aspiration, always going forward to the next goal, this inactivity, this waiting—and especially this temporary dependence on a man she didn't know—felt as if she'd said goodbye to her most trusted instincts and even her brain cells. She didn't know who this alien being was that opened her mouth and said yes to everything Armand proposed, but she didn't trust her an inch.

CHAPTER SIX

'I'M NOT coordinated. I'll fall and hurt myself. I can't do this, Armand, and especially not in the dark!'

The absolute panic in Rachel's voice was more than the natural trepidation at trying something new. Holding her close, steadying both their snowboards by keeping his at a ninety-degree angle to hers, Armand kept his voice low and soothing. 'You can't know that. We haven't even gone ten feet yet.'

'I can't even ski. How can I do this? I have no stocks. I'm going to fall. I know I will. Don't you understand? I can't go to hospital!'

He looked at her in the deep night, lit by the warmth of bagged fires on poles reflecting off the new fall of snow in small, glittering jewels. But she hadn't noticed either the night's beauty or even the fact that he'd had his arm around her waist for ten minutes. If she felt the same kind of half-amazed awakening of body and soul he experienced every time he touched her, especially since their dance and half-kiss, she wasn't showing it. She was staring down at her booted feet on a snowboard and was literally shaking.

'Have you had a bad experience in hospital as a child?' he asked gently.

She didn't even make an acid comment about his trying to psycho-analyse her, which told him her fear was very real. 'I can't be found until the divorce is final and made public. If it happens, he'll find a way to blackmail me into coming back to the show. The restraining order won't stop him. He's been losing ratings hand over fist since I left. The public now knows it was me that gave him his empathy, and that I was feeding him the answers people needed to hear. I know him—he'll be desperate by now. But he'll have a plan to win me back into his life. He's addicted to fame, and he'll do whatever it takes to make me come back.'

Now, at last, Armand got it. Really, he didn't have much choice but to understand. She was babbling her secrets in fear, secrets she'd kept chained inside her heart like a hated treasure. They'd been housemates nearly ten days now, and all this time he'd tried to get her to talk, with no success.

His arousal faded in a fit of protectiveness like a lightning-bolt, all but knocking him off his feet. His suspicions had been confirmed in a flash, and he wanted to knock Rinaldi flying—flying right off the damned planet.

Stop it. You'll terrify her. He knew that from bitter experience. He'd seen the terror on his sisters' faces on the rare times he'd been allowed home from boarding school and his father had walked in with that look on his face...

Aching to ask if she'd contacted her parents in the past few weeks, he forced himself not to reply to her secrets at all—she'd only hate him later if he did. Instead he asked, softly but in clear challenge, 'What would you say to a patient that refused to try a new experience before even attempting it?'

At that, she stilled. Slowly, she mumbled something he couldn't hear.

'I have you safe with me,' he went on, still gentle, persuasive. 'I won't let go.'

She gave a little, almost plaintive sigh. It was answer enough, since he could feel her disbelief beating from her, as strong and sure as her racing pulse.

Armand wondered if anyone had ever stayed the distance, not with her but *for* her. Had anyone ever put Rachel's needs first?

'Look around, Rachel,' he murmured to distract her. 'See how beautiful it all is.'

A small quiver ran through her. 'I can't. My eyes…'

With tenderness foreign to him until now, Armand lifted her face from the terrified contemplation of the snowboard and saw her goggles were totally fogged. 'Are you so cold?' Or worse, he thought to himself, had he frightened her into crying and not even noticed?

'I'm from Texas. It reaches freezing there in winter.'

Her semi-defiant tone, and the way she pulled her face from his hold, filled him with relief. She was a fighter, all right. 'And how long has it been since you visited in winter? LA's climate hasn't reached freezing probably since the last ice age.'

She turned away. 'Good point,' she said lightly enough, but something in her voice disturbed him.

'How long has it been since you visited Texas at all?' he asked quietly.

For a moment she neither moved nor spoke. Then she said, 'How long has it been since you visited your father's grave?'

She'd hit him with the carelessness of a drive-by shot into a crowd. How could he possibly have expected a wound so sudden and deep from a woman that until now had seemed as empathetic as she was helpless? And how could she possibly know?

Answer: she couldn't. Just as he didn't know anything about her. They were two people forced into a strange proximity, knowing only what they saw—strangers in the night, each giving the other something they needed. And that was how it had to stay. He should have known the 'defenceless kitten' thing was only part of her woman's repertoire. Her segment of the Dr Pete show proved she had far too much perception for any man's comfort.

'Interesting question,' he said, his voice calm and steady, not even a tremor to betray him. 'Now, shall we continue, or are you going to let your fears win…Dr Rinaldi?'

Her back tightened, notch by notch, even in the

heavy ski jacket. 'My name,' she said with slow, deliberate disgust, 'Is Chase.'

'Oh, I'm sorry, I wasn't certain which of your current names to call you,' he retorted in the blandest tone he'd ever used, injury added to insult. 'So has Rinaldi served its purpose? You can throw it away without regret?'

She wobbled on the snowboard as she turned fully back to him, hanging onto him for balance. Yet it didn't seem funny at all. 'The name Rhonda Braithwaite got me out of LA without his PI finding me. From Paris, I changed to Rachel Chase.' With a heavily gloved hand she pulled the goggles from her face. Her eyes were red-rimmed, watery, but she faced him from her ten-inch disadvantage with quaint dignity. 'If you'd ever had your wrist and ribs broken by someone you'd once trusted and loved, you'd know why I want to leave his name behind me—why it hurts so much to hear it. But believe me when I say I will never forget, no matter how many names I take on, or how many times I reinvent myself.'

It was a battle-axe blow to his sword-thrust— and a knockout punch for honesty. And, though he was looking into her eyes, he saw three pairs of phantom eyes beside her, behind her. Because he'd seen that look before: with Maman, Johanna and Carla when they had waved goodbye to him, the day he'd started boarding school. They'd been left alone with a husband and father who drank and gambled too much and took out his anger on his family, without their big brother to protect them.

He cursed himself in silence, then said, 'Rachel, I—'

She put up a hand. 'I've heard enough apologies lately to last me a while. Now are you going to cure me of one of my less rational fears or not, Dr Bollinger? You said something about not letting me go, I believe?'

Her eyes were twinkling now. Even though he knew it was a thin blanket covering the pain beneath, it was taking them from dangerous waters to the safer ebb-tide. So he smiled back. 'So I did, Mademoiselle Chase,' he acknowledged with mock gravity, bowing his head, sweeping a hand around them to their very private night-ski-run he'd arranged. 'But not until you have at least appreciated all the trouble I went to for you. All this beauty surrounds us, and so far you've only looked at the snowboard.'

As he spoke, he pulled out a clean tissue—when skiing, he always kept a packet on hand—gently wiped her eyes and the goggles hanging around her neck.

'Would you like to wipe my nose as well, Papa Bear?' she retorted with a loud, theatrical sniff, and he laughed. He laughed because it was cute; laughed because no woman had sniffed with him before unless it was in rage or for effect, using tears to get her way. No matter how badly he ached to take this a step further, Rachel wanted nothing from him but a skiing lesson. Despite the disappointment, it was a liberating feeling: no expectation, no neediness, just two sort-of-friends having a night-snowboarding session.

With gravity, he put the tissue to her nose and with laughing eyes she made a loud raspberry sound with her mouth, pretending to blow. They both laughed.

'Oh…'

Looking at her—what was it about her that made it so hard to look away?—he saw she was looking into the night. There was wonder in those big eyes as she took in the scattered cloud in the star-filled night, the poles with the burning bags lighting up the night, the soft-dancing snowflakes and the white-laden fir trees along the slope. And, though it was all she said, she'd made all the trouble to surprise her more than worthwhile.

'You're welcome,' he said, resisting the urge to touch that cold, snowy cheek or to bend and kiss those bitten pink lips, half-open as she drank in the night.

Had his voice sounded as hoarse as it felt to him? Did she know how much he longed to just taste her mouth once, to move his hands over her skin and see those beautiful eyes come alive for him?

Stop it. The last thing she needs right now is to start something I've never wanted to finish. I'm her emotional umbrella, nothing more. In a few weeks she'll be moving on.

For the first time, a woman would be walking away from him and he would have no choice but to let her. So, struggling to ignore the stupid physical ache to touch that was part and parcel of being a man, he swirled his snowboard around, facing down the slope with her body fitting into his, sweet and snug. He ached again and again. It felt as if the ache would never end.

Rachel; this is for Rachel. She deserves to

know there's one man she can turn to without his demands, without regrets. He had to be a better man than he'd ever been. For Rachel.

'Trust me?' he asked softly.

After the briefest of hesitations, and a tiny wobble, she whispered, 'I'm trying to.'

'I won't hurt you, Rachel.' Why did the light, teasing tone he'd employed to such effect in the past suddenly sound like a solemn vow? 'I won't let you fall.'

Her expression turned sad for a moment, even as she kept hanging onto him for the balance that seemed so elusive for her. 'There are some falls nobody can control, some hurts that can't be prevented.' Then she grinned again. 'But if I end up in hospital in traction you are *so* dead, Bollinger.'

Relieved she'd jumped back on the light, playful path, he winked at her. 'Ah, but you'd have to catch me first. Rather hard to manage from that position.'

And before she could retort in kind he moved the lower half of his body so they began sliding down the baby slope together on private, non-resort land far from the fun, romantic night-skiing he'd established years ago for his regular clients. He held her so that when she wobbled he could steady her; he moved them in as close to perfect sync as he could, slowly enough so that she wouldn't feel loss of control.

And when she was moving on her own, with her inexpressibly kissable mouth stretched in a wide smile of discovered poise and the simple joy of living, he had to move. He had no choice, really. It was move or kiss her, because if there was ever a kissing moment it was this one.

So he pulled away far enough to hold her hand. 'It's time to see what you're capable of.' After a few panicked wobbles, he said encouragingly, 'You're a natural at this. You're a snow queen. You can do this, Rachel. I know you can.'

Her astonishment, so clear even behind her goggles, and obvious in her open mouth, almost made him lose balance. 'I— Thank you. Nobody ever...' She gulped, gulped again. 'Nobody,' she whispered, and shook her head.

Nobody ever said that to me before.

And, instead of the wrong parts hurting, now it was his heart that ached for her—ached for the sweet, real 'doc with empathy' who seemed so overcome by a few words of faith. And he wished he hadn't used words he'd said before to a hundred female guests.

'It's true,' he said just loud enough for her to hear. 'Rachel, look at where you are. You *are* doing it.'

She looked down at her twisting body, at the tiny slope she was conquering. 'Oh,' she whispered, and her whole face grew alight with radiance. 'Armand, I'm *doing* it. I'm skiing.'

It wasn't the moment to correct her, or even to say that snowboarding was thought to be the harder discipline. He smiled. He smiled because he couldn't help it. His life had been dark and complicated for eighteen years and yet this woman, who was on the run from her life—a woman who'd suffered probably far more than he'd ever know—filled him with light and made him feel heartfelt bliss in this simple achievement. 'Yes, you are.'

'I feel like Lois Lane,' she said as they passed his 'start' line, making small S-slides down the slope. 'You know that scene when Superman let her fly just by holding her hand?'

'Yes,' he said, resisting the impulse to break the moment by asking if that made him Superman. She'd certainly made him feel that way.

'I feel like I'm flying, Armand.' She held onto his gloved hand as if she was about to drop off a cliff, not even realising she was all but doing everything she needed to on her own. 'You make me feel as if I can do anything.' She glanced at him; he knew because he couldn't keep his eyes from her muffled form. He felt as if he was imbibing her sparkling happiness, clear as new wine, just by being with her. 'Thank you, Armand, thank you.' Her voice was choked.

He didn't say it was nothing, because it wasn't, not to her. 'It's my privilege to be here with you, Rachel.'

'Darn, my goggles are fogging up again,' she mock-complained, trying to smile. 'Let me ski, will you?'

He laughed and said no more. It was enough for both of them.

But as they took his private cable-car back up the slope and snowboarded back down, he kept hold of her hand. He'd promised not to let her fall and she'd had enough of broken promises. And falls.

There are some falls nobody can control.

Even as he steadied her and taught her to find

her natural rhythm and ability on the slopes, the words continued to whisper to him—because she wasn't talking about physical injury.

The words haunted him because he knew she was right. Rachel wasn't fair game, and he didn't know how to be the kind of man she needed. He didn't even know if he'd want to when these few weeks were over. He was cynical, jaded, had never known how to believe in any woman outside of his family, always looking for the 'exit' sign from the night he met any woman. This awakening faith, this need to be with Rachel, was too new for either of them to trust in.

Being near her felt like touching heaven, but he couldn't let this go beyond the odd half-friendship it was now. The thought of never seeing her again, never having another night like tonight, didn't work for him. He wanted to keep her in his life. But Rachel deserved love, babies and 'for ever', and a man who could go the distance.

She deserved a man who wouldn't lash out when times got hard. Could he do that? Damn it, he just didn't know—and risking it would destroy her.

What he wanted was to be Rachel's friend—to grow older, still exchange calls, emails and cards with her—a friendship that lasted the distance. Always to have her remember him and their time together with a smile. To have her want to see him again without pain, without complications.

So he'd do his level best to stop them both from falling.

'It's simple attraction, nothing more. I am not falling for Armand. I am *so* not falling for him. I refuse to fall for him!'

Satisfied, Rachel turned from the bathroom mirror where she'd wiped a clear bit in the shower-misted glass with a wet hand. She peered at herself every morning with almost anxious paranoia, but so far she was still doing well. There were no signs of that sickly-love face she'd had during those first months with Pete. She looked happy, sure, but why not? If she still wasn't trying to get pretty for Armand—trying to lose weight or impress him with flirty banter that would never work, because she wasn't one of those waiflike models he was usually seen with—then she was safe. Safe from infatuation, nothing more.

She wasn't about to make a fool of herself over a man who was merely being kind to her. Armand deserved better than the infatuation of a needy woman he was helping out. So she wouldn't do it. Simple as that.

'Good, done. That's the way, Rachel,' she told herself, looking back for a last glimpse. No sickly-face... Oh, the relief every time she looked!

Minutes later she skipped out of the bathroom in jeans and a long-sleeved T-shirt, her hair damp and tangled. Nope, she didn't care what he thought of her looks at all. 'If you can't compete, stay out of the race', Daddy had always said.

After putting away her bathroom essentials and pyjamas—no way was she going to exasperate him by taking over his bathroom with her products or clothes!—she found him in the kitchen tossing eggs, tomatoes and mushrooms in a skillet. 'Good morning, Rachel.' He smiled at her. 'Great T-shirt,' he commented, looking at the logo. 'Where do you get your shirts?'

'I get all my T-shirts custom made.' She smiled back, convinced she'd remained cool and calm, even if he was like something from a magazine matchmaker-ad in those casual trousers and woollen pullover, cooking with supreme ease. *Let me find you the perfect man...*

'Could you butter the toast, please, and just take the coffee pot off the stove? Thanks.'

The words were so prosaic, yet so intimate. Sharing daily tasks gave a pretty illusion of togetherness. But even after that amazing night-skiing, where she'd found she could actually stay upright while she was in his hold, she refused to believe in it. Any woman would find Armand attractive, and it was no more than that.

As far as she was concerned, love was an invention of men to trap women into cooking and cleaning for them and warming their bed while they did whatever they wanted. It was a truth she'd known for a long time. If her father hadn't totally destroyed her faith in happily-ever-after, with his casual affairs and insistence on lies even when he'd been found out again, Pete had knocked all belief in fairy-tale endings from her. And he'd done it long before he'd broken her wrist. His self-absorbed use of her skills to promote his own agenda without a thought for her needs and had put her heart and her confidence in a hiding-place she'd only rediscovered since leaving him. She'd let it happen without even really noticing until it was far too late.

That wouldn't happen again. But there was no reason not to enjoy an uncomplicated friendship with Armand—especially when he'd given far more than he wanted from her.

'Butter toast and take coffee pot off the heat. Sure,' she agreed cheerfully, and pulled the toast out of the slots with careful fingers. 'Want hot milk for the coffee today?'

'I could do latte today, definitely. And there's some caramel syrup in the cupboard if you like that. I sometimes do, but usually at night.'

She gave him a quizzical grin. 'I've never met a man before that drinks all different kinds of coffee. Usually they only like one, or maybe two.'

He laughed and raised his hands, palm up. 'What can I say? I guess I'm not the faithful type, even to coffee.'

He'd been saying things like that for a few days now, hence her mirror-mantra. Though he said it too lightly to be an insult, the inference was obvious: *don't get interested.* He wasn't, and she wasn't either. Part of her wanted to blurt out that he and all men could go live and love without her caring a bit. But to put it out there would mean 'the lady doth protest overmuch'. Saying it meant she *did* care, somehow. And of course she didn't care if he found her desirable or not.

Oh, come on, who are you kidding? All people want to be attractive to everyone else. Nobody wants to be seen as unattractive. That's all it is.

With the slight discomfort of wondering if she was in denial, she found herself laughing, with a slight defiance to it. 'So you're a "serial poly-coffee-ist". It's the latest syndrome in our sad world. I'll get right onto researching it, in case you ever decide you need help.'

'Thank you,' he retorted with that grave face and laughing eyes, the hint of relief that was always there when she played his game. 'But for now I'd appreciate that hot milk more.'

She bowed and, trying to sound like a genie, said, 'Your wish is my command.'

She'd hoped to make him laugh, but as she turned away to get the milk out of the fridge, there was a bare moment when she could have sworn she saw something…

Then the moment passed, leaving her unsure if she'd seen the flash in his eyes or not. Unsure if she wanted to know. Proximity—that was all it was. It was totally natural that, if he was holed up with a woman for a few weeks, even a man like Armand would feel a passing attraction.

'Any port in a storm,' she muttered as she laid the table—and faint nausea touched her at the thought. She was no man's storm-port. She had something to give the world that had nothing to do with being a man's pretty doll, cook, house-keeper, waitress, sounding-board a child-bearer. Or career-giver and dream-provider at the cost of her own dreams. Never again.

Her endorsement deal was not the same thing. Armand was making certain her needs were being met. In return she'd give him what he wanted. Then she'd be out of here, heart and self-confidence intact.

CHAPTER SEVEN

'A *CHILL-OUT* night?' Rachel was looking at him as though he'd suddenly gained an extra chromosome instead of proposing the simplest of recreations.

Armand wasn't sure what was going on, but he went with it. 'Yes, chilling out. You ought to know the term. Americans invented it, didn't they?'

'Well, sure, of course I've *heard* of it,' she replied, sounding vaguely doubtful.

'You mean you've never done it?'

She blushed hotly, as if he'd made an intentional *double entendre*. 'I've recommended it to my patients, of course.' But the words were half-defiant, almost a question. The uncertainty was palpable in the bitten lip, the way her gaze fell to her twiddling fingers.

Without even trying or wanting to, he'd made her feel like a freak. Armand realised anew how little he knew about this woman, despite all his best efforts.

'So you're one of the world's workers,' he said with that teasing gravity that seemed to relax her. 'Let me walk you through this difficult new process, step by step.' Sweeping a hand over the living room, he winked at her. 'Here we have popcorn, chocolate, wine and a DVD—there is a choice of comedy chick-flicks, just for you. We sit on the couch with our feet up on the ottomans, eat and drink and enjoy the movie. Now, do you think that's manageable?'

If anything, her blush grew. Her smile wavered, and instead of moving to the said couch she shifted her feet until they pointed in the direction of her room. 'You must think I'm such a weirdo.' Now her shoulders turned so all of her was facing her room. She was going to bolt.

Denying her half-accusation would only make her run. 'Well, yeah,' he continued to tease. 'But, as with snowboarding, it's my honour to be your very first chill-out partner.' Again, he swept his hand to the couch, the array of inviting foods.

She didn't even look. Her gaze was firmly on her feet. 'The T-shirt says it all.' Her hand swept vaguely over her shirt. *I'm not normal*, it said.

He swore beneath his breath, trying to control

the rising anger, but the words came anyway. 'Would you like to tell me what's going on here, why you're acting as if popcorn and a movie is so wrong? This surely can't be one of your many state secrets.'

Now the blush melted down her throat and blended with her T-shirt. 'Trust me, you don't want to know.'

He laughed, but it was harsh. 'Trust, Rachel? I didn't realise that was a word in your vocabulary. I know it's only been two weeks, but frankly I'm tired of stumbling around in the dark with you. You question everything I do and say. I'm not the enemy, but I'm beginning to wonder if you see everyone as another continuation of your invisible battles. Or is it just me you treat this way?'

Her head drooped. 'Armand...'

'Don't apologise,' he interrupted her in a flat tone. 'You always do that, then you run and hide again or push me away. I'm not him, Rachel.'

A long stretch of quiet followed, and this time he refused to fill it. She either trusted him now or she didn't, and he'd give up trying. Enough was enough.

At last she mumbled, 'No, you're not him. Or

them.' Her feet shuffled, making an unobtrusive step towards the sanctuary of her room.

'Them?' he queried mildly, to make her stay. It was time.

'My family,' she muttered in a faltering tone. 'My parents and sister, Sara. I'm not like them. Nothing like them. Mama called me a change-ling—you know? The child the fairies change for another at birth. I don't look like any of them, and I don't act like them. I'm—different.'

There seemed nothing he could say in answer to that, so he waited.

Eventually she sighed, as if shedding an enormous burden. 'You see, I was a smart child. *Very* smart.'

Armand was taken aback. How could she make being intelligent sound like she was confessing to murder? 'I see.'

'No, you don't,' she retorted, lifting her face at last, her anger bursting forth without warning. 'You were *born* one of the beautiful people, the son of a movie star and a multi-millionaire. You were a movie star yourself until you retired. You were admired and loved from birth. I was a freak from the first moment I remember!'

Now wasn't the time to correct her presumptions, even if he wanted to relive his ugly childhood, picture-perfect only for the cameras. And at last she was opening up to him. 'Why?'

'I was diagnosed with an IQ of one hundred and eighty at the age of six. I finished high school at thirteen, and I had a double degree with a PhD by nineteen.'

'That's impressive,' he said, feeling his way with this, because she obviously was far from proud of her achievements.

'Oh, yes. Everyone was impressed with clever Rachel. The department came to Mama and Daddy when I was in first grade, telling them I needed special education. They put me in a special school. The boarding-school teachers loved me. The college I lived in was so proud.'

Armand frowned. 'And your parents?'

She shrugged. 'Dad was a travelling salesmanager. Mom was a doctor's receptionist. They didn't know what to make of me, where I'd got this ability from, or what to do with me when I came home. My sister Sara was pretty and popular. She liked to pretend she was an only child. Most of the time, she ignored me. I ended up spending my weekends and vacations studying at the school or at college. It was easier for everyone.'

She wasn't looking at him now, but was looking down at her feet. Shuffle-shuffle, toes stubbing against the carpet. Fingers twining around each other, or twiddling with her hair.

'When did that change?' he asked. Every question about her family seemed pregnant with tension.

She sighed. 'When I was thirteen, the teachers told them I could become a brain surgeon or a rocket scientist. I guess they thought I'd be able to support them when they retired. I did want to help people—but in a face to face way. Not with a microscope or a scalpel. I don't like blood or germs.'

'Not many people do,' he said, on a quizzical note. She sounded so ashamed of herself for that common weakness.

'Everyone said being a psychologist was a waste of my brains.' She frowned at the waiting food and drink in the living room as if it offended her. 'They only came around when…'

'When you met Dr Pete?' he prompted, sure he was right.

She sighed and nodded. 'He gave my career direction and focus. Before I met him I was working in a diner.'

'With a double doctorate and a PhD?' He was amazed.

'A PhD with a baby face,' she retorted with a shrug. 'Nobody wanted to hire me. They said no patient would take me seriously. I had to eat and pay the rent—and I wanted to study people, see what made them tick. I practised my skills on the people who wanted to talk. And then, after ten months, I met Pete—and he had enough dreams and direction for both of us.' Her voice softened. 'He took me to LA, gave me a home and a ring. He made me knock on the doors of every medical practice until I got a job. He's actually a screenwriter, you know, and has a degree in business and economics. He dreamed up the concept of the show, but we had to do a lot of study to get it exactly right. Before and after each show I had to study again, to find the right theme and make sure I had all my facts right. I—I didn't want to leave things like that to assistants.'

Repressing the urge to ask if Pete had worked at all while dreaming up the show, or if he'd used

Rachel as his meal ticket until he found fame, Armand asked, 'How did he end up the front man of the show?'

Until now he'd been too stunned to think of how much information she was giving him. He had to get as much as he could from her now, before she clammed up again.

'I threw up on the first eight attempts to put me in front of a camera.' She said it so defiantly, as if daring him to laugh at her.

Holding in a flaring urge to pull her close, he curled his fingers into his palms. Both were itching to touch her, give her comfort. 'Some people don't want the limelight, Rachel. There's nothing wrong with that.'

After a momentary glance of puzzlement, she drew a breath, bit her lip. 'When I finally stopped throwing up, I just shook so much my words mangled. So Pete said he'd take the lead, if I'd play the supporting role. I'd be back stage and give him the answers.'

'I'm guessing that worked best for you,' he said, mentally chanting, *don't touch her or she'll run.* 'So how did you end up on the show?'

'Did you like the limelight? Why did you walk

away?' she shot at him without warning, her eyes flashing.

He almost said, *this isn't about me*, but he held his tongue. If Rachel was asking, it wasn't from curiosity, but because she needed to know. 'No, I never liked it. It was a necessity at the time,' he said quietly. *Please don't ask any more.*

Those big, expressive eyes searched his for a moment, seeing too much. How she did it he didn't know, but he felt as if she looked into his eyes and down to his very soul. Eventually she nodded and moved away to sit at the couch. 'So what's the choice of movie for our chill-out night?' She grabbed a handful of the popcorn and shoved it all in her mouth at once.

It was a silent message given louder than anything Charlie Chaplin could have sent to his audience. 'I got us a range of classics. Take your pick, while I get the hot chocolate ready.'

Without looking at him she took up the three DVDs to read the blurbs at the back.

She was really good at dismissing him without a word—but, though he was willing to give her space, she'd opened the gate now. There was no shutting it again, no matter how she tried. Given what she'd said, he strongly doubted that her parents would have supported her leaving Dr Pete, even if he had been the one to break her wrist. Her sister didn't want to know her. It seemed she was an orphan adrift in the world. Someone had to let her know it was all right to be herself, that she could be liked and respected for the person she was.

And that closed the door on stupid thoughts, such as kissing her pain away.

The music of the opening credits was already running when he returned to the living room with two steaming cups. 'So, what movie did you pick?'

'*Notting Hill,*' she answered, her voice vague, humming along to the haunting sounds of She. 'It sounds lovely.'

'It— I believe it is,' he said, correcting himself just in time. 'It came highly recommended.' He sat beside her, closer to her than he'd been since the snowboarding lesson three days ago. Thigh just touched thigh as he stretched his legs over his ottoman. He didn't even know quite why he did it. It wasn't sexual provocation—even if she wanted that, he knew now he could never treat her as a casual playmate.

The truth was that he just wanted contact of some kind with her. Touching her gave him a sense of gladness in living he'd never known until now. Having a woman he desired so close but so elusive was as frustrating as it was refreshing. He couldn't seem to get enough of even the lightest contact with Rachel. The brush of his fingers against her skin when he moved a snowflake from her cheek moved him. The soft swish of her breath when she laughed intoxicated him. Inhaling her scent when she dashed by him after her morning shower was like a mint candy-cane, the ones he'd loved so much when he'd been a kid. And just holding her hand as they improved her snowboarding skills did something to him on a deeper level than he wanted to admit.

Rachel had inspired some crazy kind of yearning for the kind of relationship he'd never had before. He was yearning, waiting, but waiting less for the sexual act itself than for her to reveal her inner self to him. It felt unbearably sensual—at least for him. A situation that would no doubt end as soon as he'd…

But you're not going to have her. That's it, keep telling yourself that.

It was hard to remind himself every night when he awoke in a sweat, her face burning like a brand in his mind. Even her silly cat-pyjamas had begun to haunt him with longing.

He moved in just a millimetre, touching her more fully, and the bubbles of joy fizzled right through him. She was so close now, he could smell that wonderful candy-store peppermint scent in her hair…

She smiled up at him, but in her eyes was the slightest hint of the hunted deer, the confusion of a woman being given mixed signals. The look of a woman who doesn't want to know which signal was real: the back-off words or the touch-me body language.

He could have kicked himself again. What was he doing to her?

Forcing a smile from somewhere inside him that really didn't want to smile, he put a friendly arm around her. 'This is what friends do on chill-out nights,' he said without a quiver. With a hint of neither the laughter nor the consternation he felt in equal measure. And he hoped like hell she didn't look anywhere near his lap.

A light frown marred her brow. 'Okay,' she said,

sounding only half-convinced. Then she turned her face forward to the TV screen. 'Oh, look, the movie's starting. I really like Hugh Grant.'

The words were a nervous babble. Now his smile was genuine; he couldn't help it, she just affected him that way. She made him feel as if he was one big smile, even when he ached to...

You're asking to wake up again tonight, he thought, resigned to his immediate fate. And he spent the next hundred minutes watching Rachel more than the movie.

'No. I am not going on that thing. There is no way you're getting me on that thing!'

Swathed in his ski-gear minus the goggles as the temperature was mild today, with no wind, Armand sat on the big, wide red sled. Holding the control with one hand, he extended the other to her. His legs were splayed in an invitation to sit there that she couldn't possibly miss. 'Come on, Rachel, try it. It really is fun, and I promise you won't fall. And, if you did, it's not like there's far to go,' he laughed.

She backed off another few inches, her trepidation far greater than when he taught her how to snowboard; he had absolutely no idea why. 'No.'

His face stilled. 'You said you were trying to trust me.'

The sudden coolness in his voice made Rachel's stomach clench a bit. 'I don't want to do this. Can't you just accept it, and not push me all the time? I feel as if I'm your dolly, or your science experiment. *Let's teach Rachel something new and watch her grow,*' she snapped, not sure why she was so angry, but she was.

She turned and stomped through the snow to a crevice at the end of the tree belt on 'their' slope, isolated from the resort, totally private—as if they were in their own world.

And maybe that was the problem. It was such a beautiful lie, she almost believed it.

'Do you want to talk about what happened just now?' The gentle voice came from behind her, about an inch too close, warming her shivering skin and smelling way too good. Woodsy, strong and dependable—another beautiful, believable lie.

She moved a touch closer to the crevice. 'Do you?' she retorted, but in the same tone as his. 'Do you want to tell me why you're doing all this, being so sweet with me, trying to heal me through fun and games? I get that you *know* about me, but you're so patronising, like I'm a little kid or your sister.'

She felt rather than saw him jerk back in reaction. Without looking at him, she murmured, 'Tell me about her.' Her hand reached out to his hair, fell an inch short. Wanting it so much couldn't be healthy for her.

After a long pause, he said, 'It's not just my story to tell.'

'Okay, then I'll tell it.' She drew in a cold, pine-scented breath—a counterpoint, a denial of the ugliness she had to speak now. 'What's her name, your little sister?'

'I have two sisters. Johanna and Carla.' It came out like a gunshot. Angry and accusative: *Don't ask. Don't say it.*

But she knew better. The people who want pushing the least need it the most. 'So who beat her, Armand?' She turned to face him as she asked the question that might just push him over the edge. 'Who hurt her, that you either didn't know or didn't do anything about it? Was it her husband, her boyfriend?'

The fury was white-hot in those stormy eyes. He didn't answer, but held himself rigid, ice-like in the sub-zero day. So frozen she thought he might shatter at a touch.

'Okay, you didn't know,' she said softly, as if an admission. 'She hid it from you, didn't she? You never saw her when she had the bruises. And when she had a cast on her arm or leg she always had such a reasonable explanation for it. She might even have laughed at herself. "I'm so clumsy, Armand, you know that".'

Waiting for an answer obviously wasn't going to bring it forth, so she kept telling the story. 'And then one day there was one accident too many, was there? Or she just stopped coming to visit and didn't answer your calls. You only heard from her when she called you, when she felt strong enough. When she could control the conversation. She knew you suspected, but you couldn't prove anything.'

Nothing. Not a word or a movement. He stood like a statue, not looking at her but out into the mountains behind them. Frozen, as if it would stop her words going into his ears.

'But then one day something happened. He

went too far. He hurt her in a way she refused to accept—or she needed hospitalisation and the police became involved.'

Only the smoking heat in his eyes indicated he was alive. So pale and so cold, a beautiful statue, refusing to acknowledge anything she said.

'Is he in prison now?' she asked gently, but without remorse or pity. He had to say it. So often the victim got help but the family was left to suffer the endless guilt of not being perfect, not being able to protect the person they loved.

At last, perhaps because she just waited, watching him, he growled one word. 'Dead.'

'Good,' she said quietly. And, because it seemed right, she stripped off her glove, pulled his off too and cradled his hand in hers. It felt so right she didn't question the fact that she didn't let go after her customary thirty seconds. 'The questions don't help, you know. The what-ifs and should-have-beens never help anyone. But all you achieve by shoving them away in the back of your mind is driving yourself slowly mad with the guilt.'

He turned his face and she knew she'd hit home. 'Do you think I don't know that?'

With a silent breath of relief that he'd spoken

at last, she answered what he hadn't asked. 'No, you'll never lose the questions—but you have to deal with them, Armand, or Johanna or Carla will never stop avoiding you.'

He pulled his hand out of hers. 'You don't know what you're talking about.'

She looked at him unblinking. Slowly she lifted her imperfectly healed wrist and rubbed it: truth revealed without a word. The silent sisterhood locked in identical chains of shame.

'It was my father.' He sounded driven, half-desperate, and she knew that if anything the half-lie between them was over. From now on he wouldn't treat her as he would a sister.

A surge of hot joy washed through her. The sweet deception that he didn't know anything about her abuse, and she didn't know about his secret, had grown harder and harder to maintain. 'You ask yourself the questions, Armand—or ask me. We can talk about it, what happened to your family,' she stressed, because despite what he thought she could take care of herself. 'Tell me, Armand. Ask me all the questions you can't ask them. You have to go through it to let go of it, Armand, because they see all your pain, the regret, and it stifles them, makes them feel weak—just as this over-dose of fun does with me.'

'I just wanted to help.' The words were as cold as the ice around them.

'And you did.' The craving grew unbearable and she laid a hand on his hair. 'Don't ever doubt how much you've helped me just by being here, by letting me have my secrets. But I am not your sister.'

'I know that,' he snarled. 'I've never once seen you as my sister. As if that wasn't completely obvious to you, the way you back away from me whenever I get close.'

The anger inside those words startled her, because they seemed to come from a deeper place than wounded male ego. 'This isn't about my problem, Armand. This is about you.'

'I know that but, damn it, if she won't talk to me and won't come to me...'

'You go to her, Armand.' Oh, the stupid craving grabbed hold and wouldn't release her until she smoothed his hair, a flash of longing that only grew as she touched him. So intimate and yet it was never enough... 'You go to her after you've come to peace with the fact that you didn't stop your father. Then you accept her as she is—a survivor, even if she's damaged. Stop pretending it never happened. If you can accept her for the strong woman she is, then she can begin to feel normal at last.'

'Are you're saying I've made her feel like she isn't normal?' he demanded, leaning right over her in an open fury she'd never seen from him.

But she wasn't afraid of him. Armand would never hurt a woman physically; that she was certain about. 'If you never ask her, never talk about it, she senses that you're keeping her a victim in your mind. You unconsciously show her how much you want her to be something else by pretending the past never existed,' she said gently. 'She's been through a life-changing experience and survived it, no matter how much you or she want to forget. She isn't a victim now, Armand. She isn't a child either. She's survived suffering you can't imagine.'

He remained frozen, but the anguish in his eyes spoke for him and she began to dread that, yes, Armand could imagine it all too well, because he'd been there.

'Did you ever speak with her about it? Did you tell her how proud you are of her?'

He shook his head. 'We all just want to forget.'

'I want the moon, but that doesn't mean I'll ever have it.' When he frowned at her, so remote he might be on another planet, she tried to smile. 'We don't always want what's good for us, Armand. Talking about it doesn't just bring the monster out of the cupboard for you both—it will take your relationship to a deeper, adult level. Those horrible silences filled with fun events and determined blindness won't be needed any more.'

'I don't want to hear about her being degraded, hurt by that—' Without warning he turned and punched the tree behind him. It caused snow to fall all over them both in a tumble of freezing white, but somehow it wasn't funny. 'I don't want to know everything he did to her and I couldn't stop!'

'But you need to,' she said quietly. 'You need to take her out of that box you keep her in and allow her to be the woman she is. Until you do, you'll keep lying to each other.'

His fists clenched; slowly he turned back to her, but his eyes were closed. 'You don't know what you're saying.'

She took a breath, two, to calm herself. Then she said, 'If I don't know, who does? My parents don't want to hear. My sister refuses to believe it. Pete denies the whole abuse ever happened, and they prefer to believe I'm lying than that they could have let me down.'

The look he gave her was almost despairing, but he didn't speak.

She felt tears rush to her eyes and run down her face, cooling and making cold, salt tracks, but he'd turned away again. Instead of feeling safe, anger sizzled through her. 'I haven't pressed charges against Pete, not yet, so they *can* deny it. You have no such excuse. So let her tell you what she wants to, when she wants to, no matter how much it hurts you. *Ask her.* And you'll both heal.'

'Hell, no,' he muttered beneath his breath.

Normally at this point she'd pull back, let the person think about it before pressing her point. It was the right, the professional thing to do. She'd never later know why she lost it over the denial that was natural, human. 'Oh, for heaven's sake, Armand, *man up*!' she snarled, and then gasped at the audacity of those two insulting words. 'Otherwise you'll spend the rest of your life wishing you'd done something. Nothing is more useless than empty regret!'

Shaking off the snow, she marched past him, heading for the cabin. If he needed time to think, she'd give it to him in spades.

'Inflammatory words, Rachel.'

Before she was two steps past him he seized her, pulled her back. He moved in on her, his gaze on her mouth. His eyes were glittering, hard and dark like winter dusk. Still holding her so that she was bent backwards over his arm, his other hand pulled the hood from her head, making her hair fall around her face.

'No matter how gently I've behaved with you the past couple of weeks, you need to know I *am* a man, Rachel—and I have a man's needs.'

She gulped, staring up at him, but not in fear. Her tongue moved over her lips. 'Like what?' she whispered.

His eyes did that storm and lightning thing that made her insides flip and her femininity come to shimmering life. 'I want to know how it feels to kiss you. I've held back for your sake, but I advise you never to forget that I am a man—unless you want this kind of reaction,' he muttered against her mouth.

He really wanted to kiss her. Armand Bollinger,

noir actor and one of the world's most beautiful people... Armand her friend—her kind, wonderful friend—actually wanted to kiss her, still wanted to kiss her despite the fact that she'd just pushed and pulled his world into pieces.

The thrill that ran through her was so strong, her knees almost gave way.

CHAPTER EIGHT

'I'M STILL married, Armand.'

She was only half an inch from his mouth yet the words barely reached him, her whisper was so soft, so shaken. Her eyes were alight with heady, feminine yearning—but also with conflicted emotions. Her mouth said one thing, but her lips were speaking another language entirely. She wanted him, wanted this as much as he did.

But she'd still spoken, still said no. Although, she hadn't—she'd said *not yet*.

The thunder of his heart took a full minute to slow to something approaching normal, but his breathing was harder to rein in. His arms seized up, rebelling against his pride's need to release her immediately. 'Then don't challenge my masculinity again, Rachel Chase.'

It hurt to let go, but he did it, seconds later than he wanted to. His screaming body's need was having a hard time obeying a will fed only by his pride.

His eyes held hers, waiting for her answer. Would she be honest, or retreat into hiding again?

Her gaze dropped. 'Is that all it was to you, Armand? A challenge to your manhood—or a distraction from our conversation?' She sighed. 'I guess that makes sense, really.'

Astonished right out of his anger, he stared at her. 'You really don't know the answer to those questions?'

Her head drooped. Her eyes on her feet, she shook her head.

His hands curled into fists to stop himself from snatching her close. 'Talk to me, Rachel. Make me understand why you don't believe I could desire you.'

Her cheeks were almost scarlet, so hot they could melt snow. 'I'm not like them—the women you've been with.' Her hands lifted and fell in a hopeless gesture. 'Look at me.'

'I am looking at you. I like looking at you,' he growled, the fury flashing through him.

'Yeah, good old funny-face, like one of those

big-eyed puppies in a toy store.' She shuffled her feet in a gesture he was beginning to know well.

He snatched her close again, his eyes blazing into hers. 'That's ridiculous. Damn it, Rachel, you can't be that stupid. Half the world loves you. Surely thousands of men have desired you before now?'

She gave another plaintive little sigh, wistful, wishing. 'My fan mail was all from needy people wanting advice, Armand. Pete got the love letters, the—the propositions.'

And it seemed Pete had taken a few women up on their offers, if he was reading her correctly. Damn it. No wonder she had so little faith in herself.

'You must have had boyfriends growing up?'

She shook her head, her cheeks scarlet. 'There was nobody before Pete. He was my first everything, my *only* everything.'

First kiss, first lover—first love. The quick hot blow of jealousy was unworthy of him, when he'd had too many casual lovers to want to count. 'What has that to do with whether or not I can desire you? I still don't understand.'

Bewildered eyes met his for a brief moment.

'Nobody else ever wanted me.' With a sad little shrug she turned away, her creamy skin flushed crimson, not with cold burn.

Armand restrained the curse, but he'd never wanted to yell an obscenity more. In his entire life, he'd never had to come out of his place of emotional safety for the sake of a woman. He was always ten steps ahead of any woman he desired, ten steps nearer the door of goodbye. But sweet, damaged Rachel truly didn't understand. She truly thought herself undesirable—and if he didn't tell her now, if he headed for that door, he'd leave her for ever in that room, screaming *no man will ever want you.*

'I want you, Rachel,' he said quietly, struggling for every word. 'From the day we met, I've wanted to hold you, kiss you—and every night I fight the need to go to your room and make love to you.'

'Just proximity,' she murmured so softly he only just caught it.

The heat flaring through him loosened his stubborn tongue. 'No. Not proximity at all. It's you, only you. I've never said this to any woman before.' Unable to control it any longer, he snatched her close. The happiness that had spent a lifetime eluding him while he had tried and failed to protect his family returned in a moment's tantalising promise. It was there in the way she curved against him, in the wish so clear to read in those guileless eyes of hers. 'I've wanted you from the first, Rachel. Not because of your fame or your skills or the prospect of selling a story. You do things to me *no* woman ever has before.'

But she shook her head again. 'I can't believe this.'

Not 'don't'. *Can't.*

'It's impossible. It's a fairy tale. You might be a prince charming, but I'm no princess.'

Resisting every impulse that bid him to turn and walk now before he was in too deep, he repeated, 'Impossible, Rachel? It's impossible that I could find you beautiful, desirable? Who the hell did this to you?' Damn it, now he really *would* kill Rinaldi if he got within ten feet of the dirty jerk.

'I know what I am,' she said in a final tone, not asking for reassurance. 'Please, let me go, Armand.' She pushed at his chest.

He let her go. The pulsing beat of expectation faded to something hard and icy, leaving him feeling almost sick. 'Go on, run away,' he mocked as she stumbled past him. 'Is this my cue to say *man up*?'

She didn't even turn back. 'Probably,' she admitted sadly. 'And you'd be right.'

Frustration soared. Why did she have to be so honest all the time? 'How the hell am I supposed to answer that?'

A one-shouldered shrug showed her churning emotions. 'It wasn't a question. I'm not divorced yet. He might have cheated on me, but I won't sink to that. I won't betray myself.'

The words froze him, packed him in the kind of shame he'd never known before. He'd never touched a married woman in his life, and he could hardly believe his actions now. No matter that she was divorcing him, or that he'd abused her. Until Rachel felt free, she wouldn't be.

'Then you shouldn't have asked me, or provoked me,' he shot back, low and furious.

'I know.' She didn't apologise, didn't attempt to justify her actions, and that only made him feel lower.

This time when she kept walking, he didn't try to stop her.

Three days later

'My contract with the resort finally came through. I have to assess my new land and look at it again with my architectural designs. I'm flying in myself, over the Alps. I want you to come to the site with me and check out the progress.'

The words were stilted. He didn't want her to come. He was sticking to their bargain.

Pride warred with curiosity. She'd love to fly over the Alps. She didn't want him to think she was some kind of pushover, but flying over the Alps… The lure was irresistible. And if he truly didn't want her to come why had he given her the one piece of information guaranteed to make her fall like a ripe plum into his hand?

That decided her. If he could be brave, so could she. 'I'd love to,' she replied with the cheerfulness she'd adopted since he'd grown so stiff and cold with her.

'Be ready in twenty minutes. Bring an overnight bag,' he said curtly, barely acknowledging her acceptance. 'Do you know where the hangar is?'

She nodded. 'Do I bring my ski suit or wear it?'

'Bring it—just wear your normal clothes. It will be warm enough in the plane. The forecast over there is for cool but clear weather.' With that, he stalked out of the cabin, the tension in him ready to snap.

I want you. It's you, only you.

The words still made her shiver three days after they'd last talked, three days since he'd voluntarily spent time with her apart from meals. The power remained because, no matter how cold and even harsh he'd become with her, he still wanted her. He wouldn't be cold and harsh if he'd overcome the pain of her necessary rejection, if he no longer desired her.

But he did. Every flickered look he gave her screamed the truth in neon letters. Even in her jeans, funny shirts, no make-up and house slippers he still wanted her. And that negated the loneliness of missing him. Almost.

Twenty minutes later they were strapped in, bags stored in the cargo and Armand in the pilot's seat. 'Yes, I have my pilot's licence,' he said before she could ask. His face was still tense; for once he didn't look at her shirt with its funny logo, didn't ask. 'I'd like to visit my mother while we're there, if it suits you.'

'Of course,' she replied, hearing the wobble in her voice. He was visiting his mother only three days after their shattering scene, reliving his pain. 'I don't mind at all. But if you'd like private time with her you can leave me in the village or wherever, and I'll wander.'

There, she'd given him an out if he wanted it.

'If that's what I wanted, I'd have said so,' he replied, his whole bearing screaming 'back off, don't talk to me, don't ask'. 'I promised to care for you, never leave you alone. My mother won't mind if I bring a friend.'

For a moment she almost said the words hovering on her tongue: *am I your friend?* Right now she wasn't sure she wanted to hear the answer.

Then she frowned. 'Who's that watching us over there?'

Armand glanced in the direction of her finger. 'I don't know, but probably another guest. But don't worry; stop pointing and put these on.' He handed her a massive pair of dark lenses. 'With your shorter, lighter hair and these, let's hope whoever it is doesn't recognise you. At this distance even the best cameras would only give a grainy likeness anyway.'

'I thought I saw a flash before,' she murmured, looking at the weird sunglasses he'd given her. 'Whose are these?' Torn between amusement and indignation, she glared at him through the gold-rimmed sunglasses. 'Were these things made in the 70's?'

'Probably they were. They were my uncle's.' He shot her an inscrutable look for a few moments, then slowly a grin was born. 'You look like Fearless Fly—remember that cartoon?'

Realising he was trying to distract her, she retorted, 'I'm obviously too young to know.' When he chuckled, she poked her tongue out at him. 'You can be the Fearless Flier instead. Will you please take off?'

For answer, he checked in his flight path on the two-way, and moved the plane forward. The bright flashing light faded out as Armand lifted the small plane in the air. Was it just sunlight on somebody's glasses, or the sunlight bouncing off a camera lens or metallic edging?

She squeaked as the plane dipped and lifted. 'This is like a roller coaster. I've only flown in jumbos until now. Are the flip-flops always so bad in small planes?'

'The reactions are more intense in a small plane, because you feel every movement and bounce through every pocket of air.' As he got the plane level, he turned to her and frowned. 'Are you okay? You're looking a little green.'

Eggs and coffee were bad. Coffee and eggs were the enemy she didn't know she'd had until now. Her gaze clung to Armand's as if seeking salvation, but her breathing shook with every bounce of the little craft. Too many air pockets; eggs and coffee were burning in her stomach, rising to taunt her…

'Here.' With a terse word, an open bag was pushed into her hands and, grateful beyond words, she lurched forward.

A few minutes later, she finally emerged from the second air-sickness bag, trembling and with involuntary tears streaming down her cheeks. 'Just as well we're just friends. If I was one of your normal women wearing all that make-up, I'd look like a clown by now,' she joked, croaking.

He turned his face to hers, his expression gentle for the first time in three long, lonely days. He used a wet tissue to wipe her face, to clear the wetness on her cheeks. 'You're not like them in any way.'

He didn't say if it was a good thing or a bad thing, but she didn't want to ask. Her loud, undignified display had spoken for itself: she was nothing like them.

I don't want to measure up to them. I knew all along that thinking of anything between us but friendship was a bad idea. I don't want anything else!

And on that uplifting thought she sat huddled away from him in miserable silence—unless turbulence would force her to croak, 'Bag,' again.

Eventually exhaustion claimed her. She drifted in and out of sleep, woken up only when she had to embarrass herself again. Apart from flying the plane and handing her ginger-mint tablets to help settle her stomach between bouts, Armand remained still and silent. No doubt he was counting his blessings that she'd rejected him every time he heard her retching again. *Please, God, let this torture soon be over!*

'Rachel.'

She jerked awake at the sound of his voice. 'Sorry,' she murmured through the fog clouding her mind.

'Don't be. I'm glad you slept,' he said quietly. 'I thought this might cheer you up.' He pointed just ahead of them, then down and all around. 'We're flying over the French Alps.'

She gazed over the window and a gasp escaped her lips. She'd been totally inspired, seeing the Swiss Alps coming in on the TGV train from Paris. But seeing the French Alps from above like this struck her with awe, with their unending, snow-capped magnificence. 'Oh…it's like a new world,' she breathed, just holding back from pressing her nose to the window as Armand turned the plane south. 'It's the most beautiful thing I've ever seen.'

'That's what I've always thought.' He smiled at her, the tense silence between them seeming to vanish along with her stomach contents. 'We just crossed the border. The airport is in France—we're about to land. We'll cross back into Switzerland to reach the land and my mother's house.' He handed her another bag. 'This will be the last time you'll need it, I hope. We'll be taking my Range Rover from here.'

'France,' she breathed again, feeling like the rawest *ingénue* and not caring. The romance, the magic of it grabbed hold of her sore and embarrassed heart, filling it with happiness. 'I'm in *France*.'

'I gather that thought makes all of your suffering worthwhile?'

She nodded, her eyes shining. At this moment, it was worth everything. This was her first sight of France in daylight. She'd arrived in Paris the first time by night and, under the threat of someone recognising her at the time, had just bolted for her seat on the fast train to Zurich. But this was pure, uplifting loveliness, one perfect, snow-capped peak after another filling her senses to overflowing.

'We're heading for the landing strip at the base of Chamonix. Hold on tight, we need to lose altitude quite quickly to land.'

He didn't have to tell her that. Her stomach had announced the descent with a brass band at the first drop in height. With a wretched groan, she forgot she was in magical France and the magnificent Alps, shoved her face in yet another clean air-sickness bag and kept it there until the plane was completely still in a darkened hangar.

'We're here. Though it's only autumn, we're five-thousand feet above sea level, so it's quite cold outside even if it isn't snowing. You'll need your jacket and gloves.' His prosaic comment, without the patronising gentleness that had irked her before, soothed her frayed nerves. 'Take your time. I'll bring the car to you.'

She didn't move or answer even with a nod. The landing had been the worst, filled with sudden dips, and all she could think about was the reasons she'd never returned to any of the theme parks in LA after her first time.

Roller coasters and light planes were the pits.

Her mind remained venomously on that thought until the lovely, wonderful Range Rover with its smooth suspension and travel on blessed ground pulled up beside the plane. Only then did she move. Wary of every step, she hung on to anything she could as she headed towards the midsection where the stairs were.

Armand met her halfway up the stairs. 'You aren't wearing— Ah, I see. Let me,' he said, still crisp and practical, and put her trembling arms into the snug warmth. He zipped it up and put the hood over her head, encasing her in sweet heat. 'Come, I'll help you to the car.'

Just as well for, though her pride rebelled, her

body had given up the ghost; she was so weak she could barely move alone. She leaned on him down one stair, two, then he swung her up into his arms and carried her to the open passenger seat. 'I've ordered a thermos of peppermint tea for you for the trip. You'll feel better soon.'

She couldn't even thank him, but her hand caught his and clung for a moment.

'You're welcome,' he said softly, with a smile that told her everything he'd done was no big deal and he wasn't at all disgusted by her weakness. Rachel sagged against the leather upholstery in relief. Having a man care for her needs without ridiculing her for it was such an amazing experience, she hardly dared believe Armand was real.

The psychologist in her had always understood why Pete had felt the need to put her down—he'd felt threatened by her intelligence and her superior knowledge of psychology, and then by her ratings. But the woman and wife had never quite managed to come to terms with it. She'd just felt unwanted, unloved, not pretty enough, too clever—always too much and not enough.

And that was why the man currently putting himself out to get her peppermint tea was so dangerous to her emotional well-being. A millionaire in shining armour. Maybe he was just superb at making all women feel special, beautiful and adored—she'd bet he was, given how women constantly fell at his feet. But that was her problem, not his. After so many years with someone who made her feel unworthy, every moment with Armand gave her a feeling of teetering at the edge of a precipice. She kept waiting to fall, only to smash to the ground when he moved on.

She started when he bent over her, pressing a thermos and cup into her hands. 'Pour only small amounts at a time and sip slowly. The honey will help you, but it could be too much if you gulp.' He poured a small measure of tea into the plastic cup. 'I think we should get your stomach settled a little before I drive.'

She stared at him in wonder over the rim of the cup as she sipped. 'Your mother's waiting for us.'

'Don't worry about that. She'll understand.' Then he smiled and pulled out his phone. 'Okay, I can see you're worried. I'll call her now, if that will reassure you.' He punched numbers into the phone and spoke in rapid French to his mother, in a dialect she couldn't quite grasp. Rachel sipped more tea and felt like the world's biggest nuisance. Why wasn't he ready to ditch her somewhere and get on with his high-flying, jet-setting life? Surely it was obvious by now she wasn't the kind to fly anywhere with him—literally.

'My mother wants to speak to you.' He handed her the phone.

In still greater wonder, Rachel prepared herself to talk to a woman any talk-show host would sell their grandmother to contact: the luminous, every-award-in-the-world winning, reclusive actress Claire Tessin-Bollinger. 'Hello, Mrs Bollinger?'

'Hello, Rachel, please call me Claire. Armand told me how you suffered on your first trip in a light plane. I well remember my first time. I think I went through seven air-sickness bags.' The warm, thrillingly accented voice that had haunted generations of movie-goers walked through a little crack in Rachel's heart, and she loved the older woman instantly without having met her.

'Yes, I was pretty sick,' she managed to croak in reply, unable to believe the exquisitely beautiful Claire Tessin had ever been airsick. She was probably just reassuring her but, oh, she felt so much better, just hearing it. 'I'm so sorry to keep you waiting.'

'Please don't worry about it in the least. Time is in no way imperative for me. Go and see the land with Armand, and come here when you're done. A little time in the fresh air ought to revive you. And I look forward to meeting you, no matter what time you come.'

Rachel's heart totally melted at the comfort. 'Thank you,' she whispered, struggling against tears of overwrought relief. 'I'll see you soon.'

She handed the phone back to Armand. 'She's so lovely.'

'Feel better now?' he asked simply, as if that was his primary concern. She bit her lip and gulped. Too handsome, too kind, too perfect... Why did he care if she felt better?

'Yes,' she whispered, wishing he'd go away and leave her, wishing she'd never wake up from this lovely dream. This couldn't be her life. A man like Armand Bollinger could never have said, *I want you, only you.*

'Good.' He leaned over her, checking her seat-belt. His gaze met hers, so tense and dark it sent a hot thrill through her, negating the illness. 'We should go.'

No words came to her choked throat. She nodded.

After he clipped himself in the car, he said, 'Oh, I forgot, I have a present for you.' He tossed her another sickness bag, this one emblazoned with a sticker saying, 'Rachel'.

And just like that the shadows of tension and aching desire vanished. 'You can't tell me the shop had sick bags with stickers on them?'

He grinned at her and started the car. 'No, I had the bag already. They sold the name stickers, though. It was my own invention.' His smile was full of too-innocent pride.

'Oh, you rat. You must've driven your sisters crazy,' she laughed, putting her Styrofoam cup in a holder. 'Where's the wolfish beast I met nearly three weeks ago?'

His grin grew, reminding her of the Cheshire Cat. 'Does it matter? What's important is that you're no longer wondering whether your breath smells of vomit or peppermint.' He winked at her when her mouth fell open in half-amused indignation. 'And I'll never tell.'

Rachel rolled her eyes. 'Oh, you were a holy terror as a boy, for sure. I'll bet your sisters hated you.' And as another shadow touched his face she added hastily, 'Let's go. I don't want to keep your mother waiting any longer than we need to.'

The road was steep and winding, but Armand drove with careful precision. It was obvious he knew the road well, and he warned her whenever they approached a bend. Rachel didn't talk the entire trip. Though the view was almost heartbreakingly beautiful, her stomach still burned and ached and the weakness was slow to leave.

But when they stood in the fresh, clear mountain air surrounding his proposed resort she soon forgot about feeling sick.

The land Armand had bought for his resort was on the far edge of a village. But, though the temperatures hovered just above freezing, the land was much further down on its mountain and there was no snow as yet. Winter hadn't arrived here, early or otherwise. It was sloping, mountainside land, unfit for farming, but covered with the heather-like flowers called Edelweiss, and other little flowers, red and blue. Deep square holes littered the slope, surrounding a natural rock pool, curling steam rising gently from its surface.

Armand turned to her, his expression too reserved to be real. 'What do you think?'

Understanding what her endorsement meant to him, she stuttered, 'It's—it's exquisite. But…the flowers…'

'They're indigenous plants, Rachel, and very hardy. What we dig up, we're going to replant—but because this resort will have hillside chalets on poles, it means there will be very little environmental impact. Given that this will be a wellness spa-resort rather than a ski resort, it has to be environmentally friendly to sustain the water source.' From the back seat of the Range Rover he pulled out rolled-up blueprints. 'This is what I have planned.'

Standing beside him, the unrolled blueprints in his long-fingered hands, she felt the intimacy of the situation. But that was ridiculous! This was part of his business contract, no more. *And no doubt I still smell of vomit!* She shook herself mentally, pushed wayward, wind-blown strands of hair from her face and forced herself to look.

'Oh, it's lovely,' she murmured, conscious not to breathe too hard.

True to his promise of exclusivity, there were only three-dozen chalets, all on poles for minimal environmental impact. They surrounded the spa, which would be rock-lined instead of tiled like a traditional pool. Above and around the pool would be the wellness centre, built again for minimal damage.

'As I hope you can see, there is no gym, no conference centre, not one building that will take away from the natural beauty of the place. That's why I fell in love with the land here.' He smiled. 'This is my mother's childhood village.'

Her brow crinkled. 'But doesn't your sort of clientele demand luxurious facilities?'

'Yes, they do. That's why there will be plenty of luxury transportation to the fully equipped facilities right on the furthest edge of the resort. It will be just over half a mile away so they can jog right down our own private road.' He pointed at the building near the proposed gate. 'This will be our wellness-fitness resort, so those who come here will presumably not be the kind to want a shuttle on hand to ride everywhere, but I will of course provide for such a request in case.' He glanced at her, then away. 'So, what do you think of it?'

Without hesitation and in total honesty she replied, 'I think you'll make everyone happy with this resort, Armand. It's a wonderful proposal—and, yes, it's definitely one I'd be happy to endorse. You've made it easy to love.' She grinned up at him. 'Can I be one of your first guests? Is there a waiting list yet?'

'Not yet, but I promise you, your name will be the first on it.' His smile was one she hadn't seen from him in days. No strain, no forced stretching of his lips, but genuineness, relief. No tension, no memory of her rejection. 'Thank you, Rachel.'

As they walked back to the car, he said, 'Maman has invited us to stay the night. I accepted on your behalf. I thought it best that you don't fly again until tomorrow.'

His voice was a shade too casual. The mask was back in place. He didn't know if she'd trust him, or would dig for deeper reasons why he'd answered for her. 'Thank you,' was all she could find to say that wouldn't take them back to a place where neither of them wanted to be. 'I think that would be best, as well, unless you have another dozen sickness-bags with my name on them.'

'No, not quite so many as that. I think I should stock up for tomorrow.' But his military-straight shoulders had relaxed a fraction, and he handed her back into the car with his customary courtesy.

Soon he pulled up in front of a picture-perfect, white house hundreds of years old that wasn't quite big enough to be a real château, but was warm and welcoming, with snow on the dark-red roof, window sills and hand-carved shutters with flower shapes at their heart. 'Oh, how lovely,' she breathed. 'I grew up in a nice house in the suburbs, all new, with straight picket-fences and laid-out gardens.'

'It is beautiful. This house has some pretty views of Chamonix, Mont Blanc and the valleys from the south windows. No, don't try to get out alone. You may not be steady yet.' He came round the Range Rover and helped her out of the car. He kept his arm around her as they headed up the thirty or so stairs to the front door. 'You're still shaking. I should have taken you to see the land after you'd had something warm to eat.'

'Food?' Rachel shuddered, trying to resist

the urge to lean against him. When she left Switzerland, she needed to be strong, able to stand as she faced Pete, his barrage of lawyers and their agent. But for now Armand's care was a healing balm on years of raw wounds, and that much she would accept. 'I don't think so.'

'Don't worry. If I know Maman, she's made something your stomach can tolerate. She's suffered from air sickness all her life, especially in small aircraft.' When she faltered two-thirds of the way up, he lifted her into his arms and moved carefully up the final few stairs. He held her close after he put her down to press the bell. 'You're too shaky to stand for now. I'll go back for the bags once I've made certain you're comfortable.'

She looked down, but the mantra wouldn't come to her lips this time. She had to deal with this, cut her feelings off at the knees before she fell on them, literally. 'Please stop this.'

His finger was about to press the bell and he frowned at her. 'Stop what?'

He acted as if he really didn't know. Aiming for strength when she was already shaking, she said as steadily as she could, 'I've said I'll do the endorsement, okay? So stop doing all this—taking care of me. Making me feel as if I'm important to you. I know it's probably just what you do with women in general, but it—it isn't right.'

'What I do?' He released her. 'Would you care to explain that remark?'

He spoke quietly and she thought of his mother, who could be on the other side of the door. 'Isn't that why women fall at your feet, because of this? This ingrained courtesy you have? The wonderful manners? I'm sure your mother taught you, she seems a wonderful woman. You have younger sisters, one of whom…' She bit her lip. 'I remind you of her. I'm sure you want to—to redress the universal scales.'

His chuckle took her by surprise. 'Do I? Do I seem like some sort of new-age guru?'

Frustrated, she tried to square up to him—hard to do when she was shaking like a leaf and so very aware of his advantage of geography as well as height. 'Isn't it why one of your women called you the Wolf?' she demanded. 'You're strong, supportive, so very charming…but beneath all that you're a loner. There's always the door in front of you. It—it isn't right.'

'That isn't why I'm called that. Not at all.' The

smile had faded during her mini-tirade; now there was nothing left of it, just those fathomless eyes in a face sculpted from cold stone. 'What isn't right, precisely?'

Rachel felt like a balloon with the air being slowly let out—deflating, making useless squeaking sounds. She looked at her feet and mumbled, 'You treat me like I'm a princess. I'm not used to it, Armand. I don't want to…become dependent. I'm leaving soon. I need to stand alone.'

A long silence ensued. 'You think I'm weakening you.' It was a flat statement, angry.

'I don't think you mean to.' She hesitated, looked up and saw a perfect mirror for his tone in his eyes, and suddenly had no idea what she'd been going to say. 'It's just that you're so kind, so perfect…' Her words trailed away. She wanted to squirm.

Dragging in harsh, uneven breaths, he snarled, 'So I seem perfect to you? Well, perhaps you'd be more comfortable if I—' He shook his head and said no more but she knew: *if I treated you as Pete did…*

Jerking back without meaning to, she hit the doorbell with her elbow. With a tiny, mewing sound of pain, she felt his hand on her arm, helping her.

'Stop it!' she cried. 'I'm not a kitten stuck up a tree in your backyard, Armand. Don't try to rescue me unless I ask for it!'

'Oh, I beg your pardon,' a soft, musical voice said with a charming accent. Rachel started and pulled out of Armand's arms, feeling the blush burning her whole face and her heart free-falling to her feet. Could there be a more embarrassing way to meet a man's mother?

CHAPTER NINE

RACHEL could barely look into the tall, white-haired, elegant beauty that was Claire Tessin. 'Oh, I'm so sorry, *Madame*. Um, I was just… We were…'

Claire broke into laughter, bright and golden. Slowly, Armand's deep laugh mingled with his mother's, mirth without malice, like distant bells tolling together. 'She knows what we were doing, Rachel.' He lifted his mother's hand in his and kissed it. 'Maman, it's good to see you,' he said in French. 'Obviously, this is Rachel. Rachel, this is my mother. Rachel's fluent in French, Maman.'

'Ah, but I don't practise my English enough,' Claire replied in English, smiling at a still-blushing Rachel. 'Please don't feel uncomfortable, Rachel. We all have our disagreements.' She ushered them inside the house and down a thin hallway lined with ancient doors to the living room at the back of the house. 'How are you feeling now?' The older woman looked at her face. 'I do not think you are always so pale. You did not eat yet?'

'I'm really not hungry, *madame*,' Rachel said with as much firmness as she could.

'Ah, but I have long experience with my enemy, *la maladie de l'air*. You will not feel better until you have eaten, I promise you. I've made a tomato and mint soup, with a hint of ginger. I always found it helpful after my ordeals in the air.'

'I knew I could count on you, Maman.' Armand hugged and kissed Claire. 'Rachel's had quite a bad time of it today.'

'I think she and I had much in common.' Claire turned back to Rachel, waving towards an old, pretty settee in faded pink and cream. A small mahogany table stood in front of it, laden with teapot, milk, sugar and cups. 'Pour the tea, Armand. Please make yourself at home here, Rachel. The tea will help you recover, so we can have a comfortable lunch on the settee where you can rest.'

Rachel sat, staring at the slim, upright figure as she left the room. 'She doesn't have servants to do this kind of thing?'

'Of course,' Armand replied simply. 'A housekeeper and gardener for the heavy housework that's beyond her now. But Maman prefers to cook and take care of herself whenever she can. She's always loved to cook, and her kitchen garden is her passion. The soup will be full of herbs she grew herself.'

After ten years in Tinsel Town, she could barely comprehend a woman of Claire's fame doing the cooking, gardening or any kind of cleaning. 'No wonder you're so…normal,' she finished, feeling idiotic saying it, but no other word came to mind. 'Your mother raised you to be just like other people, didn't she?'

'We *are* like other people,' he reminded her in a tone of steady gravity. 'I actually am a normal human being, as hard as that is to believe.'

'That's not what I meant.' But he passed her the tea he'd poured, unable to clarify what she had meant. She sipped at the cup; the tea was made with just a little milk and sugar, as she liked it.

He'd even noticed how she took tea.

'Maman did her first feature film when she was twenty,' he said when she continued drinking her tea, feeling the final residue of pain in her stomach and throat slowly subside. 'She saw the children of the other actors brought along with their nannies and tutors, children who either threw tantrums to get attention or were unnaturally well-behaved, and she decided that when she had children she would retire to raise them and give them as happy and normal an upbringing as possible. My father also did not want us to be brought up in the limelight.'

'I see,' she murmured, noting that Armand never once called his father anything but that—'my father'. Formal and cold.

'My father came from a very wealthy, upper-class family. They didn't want him to marry an actress. But instead of getting nannies and servants Maman left her career behind to raise us herself and to support my father's career. She'd spend days in the kitchen cooking when we had visitors. She only agreed to an au pair during the times when my father needed to take her on a business trip. So, while we are the children of wealthy parents, we've had what most people would consider a normal, if privileged, childhood.'

He had a strange look on his face—far away, as if he spoke of someone else's life. 'Was this your home?' she asked in a near-whisper, half-afraid to shatter the moment.

'Our holiday home, yes, for summers and ski week,' he answered, still wandering in the halls of happy memory. 'We lived most of the time in Geneva, though we lived two years in London, and we spent one memorable year in Manhattan where our accents and life made us exotic to the other kids. We were all pretty popular, but I think that was more because of Maman. There were a thousand cameras at the school every time Maman came for an event.'

'I'll bet there was. You've led such an international life,' she murmured with all the wistfulness in her heart. Again she noted that something missing—his father. 'It sounds so wonderful, so... sophisticated.'

'Yes and no,' he said, but jumped to his feet as his mother brought in a tray laden with soup and bread. 'Let me do that for you, Maman. Carrying all that weight can't be good for your arthritis.'

As Rachel quickly took the placemats from the tray Armand held and helped him set the table, she could see any explanation would have to wait for another time. Not that she'd believe the 'no' part. A childhood spent in Geneva, Chamonix, London and New York... What couldn't be wonderful about that? She felt like a backwoods provincial next to the Bollinger family.

'This soup is divine,' Rachel mumbled as she gulped her first mouthful. 'You're a gifted cook, *madame*—um, I mean, *Claire*,' she added in haste as Claire mock-frowned.

'Necessity is the mother of invention, isn't that what they say?' Claire rejoined, smiling. 'Not only did I need this soup after a flight anywhere, but I learned to cook in self-defence. On the set, there was a choice of ordering in, going to another restaurant with a high chance of being mobbed when you were exhausted after a long day's work, or I could eat in. So I bought cookbooks.'

'And discovered her true vocation,' Armand put in, deadpan, his eyes dancing. 'We never ate out anywhere as kids if she could help it.'

'I don't notice you turning the food down,' Rachel retorted. 'Or ordering in.'

He did that elegant shrug she always wished she could emulate. 'Would you, if your mother served you ambrosia?'

'My mama makes the best macaroni and cheese ever.'

His brows lifted in a mock-impressed expression. 'Would she consider living in Switzerland, catering to the American guests I hope to draw here?'

Rachel snorted. 'She's never been on a plane in her life, and every ship is potentially the *Titanic*. She's always been afraid of travel, except by train or car.' She tilted her head at him, with a challenging grin. 'But I know the recipe, I'm not a bad cook, and I need a new direction. Think there's a future for me with the Bollinger chain?'

'I'd have to do some serious taste-testing first,' he said with a straight face, but his gaze rested on her mouth for a moment and she felt heat scalding her cheeks.

Claire's eyes were gentle on them, one to the other. 'You're obviously recovering, Rachel.'

Completely recovered, in fact, she thought in wonder. 'It's this incredible soup—and all the tea I've been given in the past hour. Though I'd appreciate knowing where the bathroom is at this point,' she added, her blush intensifying, though why it did she had no idea. It felt ridiculous to think that a goddess like Claire Tessin would need a bathroom. She was one of the favoured few who probably did roll out of bed not only beautiful but elegant, perfect.

I'll just bet Armand does, too, she thought with an inner sigh.

'Rachel?'

She started and turned to see Claire on her feet. 'Come with me.' Feeling like an idiot, Rachel jumped to her feet and Claire led the way back down the hall and opened a door. 'Take your time.'

'Thank you. You've—you've been so kind to me,' Rachel faltered. It was strange to realise that when her sister, long-time friends and her husband had all let her down when she needed support, strangers from another continent had taken the role.

'You're welcome, *chérie*. You're good for my son,' Claire said softly. 'No wonder he brought you here to me.'

'No, no, that was to help me. It's just a business arrangement…' Rachel felt herself blushing again as she remembered how Claire had caught them arguing at the front door. 'I mean…' What did she mean? She'd gone blank as she'd discreetly hopped from one foot to the other, in pain but trying to be polite.

Claire smiled at her. 'What am I doing, keeping you here? We can discuss this later—but you should know, Armand has brought no other woman to meet me in the past fifteen years.'

'Um, okay, thank you.' Desperate now, she closed the door behind her.

It was only when she was washing her hands that the force of Claire's words struck her. Why had he brought her here? To gain time to think, she washed her face and rinsed her mouth but, try as she might, no reason came to mind…apart from the dreaded novelty-value.

Facing herself in the mirror, she knew it was that; it had to be the truth. No matter what euphemisms had been used to describe her puppy-dog eyes and way-too-big smile by the media during her brief brush with fame, sitting in a freckled face and plain brown hair, she looked exactly what she was: a dumb country girl with a growing crush on her smooth, sophisticated opposite.

Her mouth fell open when she realised what she'd just accepted, if only in her mind. She had a crush on Armand.

Oh, no. This had disaster written all over it. Calamity Jane meets Cary Grant; the prince enchants the Vegas ticket-booth girl; The sheikh hangs out with the checkout chick. A beautiful fantasy, but a happy end was never going to happen.

'Rachel, are you all right?' It was Armand, his voice filled with concern.

Pulling herself together with a final splash of very cold water on her face, she called, 'I'm fine.' She opened the door with a bright smile. 'I *really* had a lot of fluid, you know.'

He chuckled, apparently willing to forget their argument for now. 'You lost a lot of fluid, too. I know, I had to dispose of it.'

Darn the man! It was when he was at his most ordinary that he took her breath away. 'I never promised you a rose garden,' she sang flippantly. 'I'm sure disposing of air-sickness bags was in the contract I signed.'

As she passed him, he took her hands in his and turned her to face him. His eyes were serious. 'Being with you is no hardship, Rachel. I haven't had this much fun in years—and that's the truth.'

Heart pounding and her blood racing like a go-kart downhill, she stammered, 'Sure—sure you have.' *Keep it cool, keep it together. He doesn't know what he's doing to me.*

'I told you not to challenge me, Rachel,' he said, soft with intent—and, before she could stop him, his mouth had brushed hers.

A moment's touch, but she'd suddenly lost the ability to speak. 'I…'

'I know,' he whispered against her mouth. 'It's all right. I wouldn't try anything in my mother's house. I brought you here because I knew she'd like you—and to show you how much I respect you. But I warned you before, don't challenge me, Rachel. It's asking for trouble.'

Her breath was stuck in her lungs and her knees were trembling. She nodded and forced herself to pull away. She kept her eyes closed for another moment. *Don't say it, not here in his mother's house. She actually thinks he cares about me.* 'No, definitely not kosher to do this in your mom's house, Bollinger,' she whispered, making herself smile up at him. *Like the kiss was no big deal for me. Like the sight of his face, my kiss still on his lips, doesn't make my knees weak and fill me with yearning for more.*

'Not gentlemanly of me at all, but I feel a little savage right now.' And he yanked her back to him.

'Believe in yourself, Rachel, or you'll force me to desperate measures.'

She felt more feeble by the moment, as her body cried out, *more, more.* Her battered heart grew little tentacles, wanting to hold him to her with unseen suction-cups. *Stay with me, please stay with me.*

That did it. She tore herself from his arms and shook all the way to the settee, which was blessedly empty. 'No more, Armand. It's been a hard few months. Please, give me space.'

The desire and need faded from his face and the thundercloud behind the sunshine that had taken her breath the first time they'd met returned in full force. 'Why don't you tell me what it is I'm doing that's so wrong?'

She shook her head. 'Not here, in your mother's house.'

'Maman knows we're both adults.'

She really didn't want to do this now, but he'd been the one to push her into it—and she had to say something now or regret it later. 'You've played the game for years with some of the world's most beautiful women. But I'm not one of them. I barely know the rules. I might be almost divorced, but I don't *feel* free yet. I still don't know what I want to do with my life, and I don't want to become the latest woman in a long line of Armand Bollinger's exes while I'm waiting to find out.'

The frown deepened between his brows. 'I've looked after you for over two weeks, shown you my hopes and plans—I even brought you to meet my mother—and you still think I treat you as if you're only a bit of transitory fun for me?'

He folded his arms, waiting for her answer, dark, angry, serious and beyond beautiful. She sat staring at him, enthralled, aching. Why did he *care*? 'I'm nobody's transitory fun,' she whispered. 'I don't know how to be.'

'Oh, I think you do. Don't play the country-girl card now. I've seen your show once or twice. I heard you give all your sage advice on healing through transitional people.' He stood over her, angry yet without threat. Even now, he wouldn't intimidate her to make his point. 'I'm beginning to wonder if you've been the one who's playing me all along, all alone and sweet and helpless to get your way.'

The truth of his words felt like being hit by a baseball bat for a home run. She felt shocked, appalled. But she said, 'You're right, I know what it is in theory, but I've never done it.'

'Oh, I think you have. I think you've been practising on me. What am I, your safe person because I don't have feelings? I don't get hurt, is that right?'

Again, he'd knocked it out of the park. Too handsome, too perfect—had she treated him as the Wolf, or as a real man?

She laced her fingers together tight. 'If I was doing that, I didn't know. I *was* alone, Armand. All I could think about in LA was escape, and I did—but when you arrived in your resort that day, I didn't know what to do. It was you that just took over.' Biting her lip, she drew in a breath and said simply, 'I understand if you want me to go.' Rising onto legs that still quivered, she walked to her bags, sitting against the back wall of the lovely, bright room. They felt like ton weights in her hands. 'Please thank your mother—and thank you, Armand. Thank you from the heart, for everything you've done for me,' she said quietly.

Armand swore in fluent French. 'Damn it, Rachel, you can't leave like this.' He strode over and pulled the bags from her. 'I'll see this through. I gave you my word.'

Trembling deep inside, she lifted her chin. 'I release you from your promise. And don't worry. I'll still endorse your resort.' Then she gulped. 'I didn't mean to—to use you, Armand, but you made it impossible to say no.'

'I suppose I did.' To her surprise, he gave her that rueful smile she couldn't resist. 'You're as confusing as hell, you know that? Every time I think I have a handle on you, you spin me around until I'm dizzy.'

A smile of pure relief curved her mouth. He wasn't angry any more and she shrugged. 'Sorry?' It came out as a hopeful question.

'All I wanted was to keep going as I was, making greater successes with my resorts, finding new ventures to build up from the ground,' he muttered. 'I was satisfied with my world. Then you came into it and turned everything upside down in minutes.'

'I seem to have a talent for that,' she admitted. It certainly resembled the shambles she'd created of her life. Calamity Jane had struck again.

Armand stopped the pacing he'd begun with his last pronouncement and threw her a searching glance. 'Stop it. Stop apologising. Stop blaming yourself for everything.' Suddenly he had her hands in his, refusing to let go even when she pulled and tugged. 'I could have walked away that first day, let you leave my resort and my life. You weren't trying to stop me. You've never asked a single thing of me. I've made all the moves.' He lifted her chin so he could look down into her eyes. 'I stopped you when you wanted to go it alone. I did all this, Rachel. It's my decision. I accept the consequences.'

Completely taken aback, she blinked at him but didn't find words. She blinked again, wondering if she was awake or dreaming.

He saw it, and his face softened even as he frowned. 'Has anyone ever said that to you before, Rachel? Just accepted the consequences for their own acts?'

'I don't think so,' she whispered. Somewhere deep inside a trembling began, the one that told her this was a big moment. Big. Life-changing. 'I mean, Mama and Daddy weren't like that, not really. Only once or twice, but those times were my fault...'

Softly, his fingers moved against her skin, sending tiny warm shivers through her. 'How long have you been accepting the blame for other people's decisions that turned bad?'

At first, all she could hear was the echoes of the past in the present: *am I Armand's decision gone bad?* Then she heard what he'd said. 'I don't know,' she mumbled.

'Months? Years? All your marriage—or all your life?' he pressed, his expression telling her he wouldn't let this go.

Rachel opened her mouth, and closed it. 'I don't know.' But it sounded horribly familiar, a song she'd been singing too long. *I'm sorry, I'm sorry...*

I'm sorry, Mama and Daddy, but I don't want to be a doctor or a rocket scientist.

I'm sorry, Sara, she'd said when all Sara's beautiful friends had laughed at her for having such a nerdy sister. And she'd run away, back to the college she'd been attending since she was fourteen, safe from ridicule, but so alone. She'd even apologised when Sara had said she had her bridesmaids picked out, and Rachel wasn't one of them. *I'm sorry I'm so plain and awkward.*

I'm sorry, Pete doesn't want babies yet, she'd said whenever her parents had nagged for Rinaldi grandchildren. *The show takes all our time. You have Sara's kids, right?*

I'm sorry I'm not taller or prettier, Pete.

I'm sorry I'm smarter than you want me to be. I'm sorry I'm not as pretty as the women you meet at the studio. I'm sorry, you were wrong on what you said to that person in the audience—you'll need to retract it, I'm sorry...

She'd even apologised to Pete when he had been in the wrong.

She'd apologised to Sara ten years later, apologised to already divorced, very rich Sara who'd complained bitterly when Pete had left her, Rachel, for Jessi... It was so embarrassing to have a famous sister that was such a loser.

I'm sorry, she'd cried wretchedly when Pete had said the least she could do for him was swallow the story he'd sold to the tabloids, and let him get on with his career. She didn't want to destroy the show, did she? Could she ruin a hundred and fifty families and shatter the million fans that depended on Dr Pete's continuance?

Armand had presented her with the big moment, the life-changing question—and she was a total failure as a psychologist because she had no answer. At least she had no answer she was prepared to give him, not to the smooth, confident, perfect Armand Bollinger. A wavering hand moved to her eyes. 'I—I think I need to sit down.'

'You've turned white. Come here.' But she couldn't make her knees work, so Armand came to her instead, lifted her into his arms and carried her back to the settee. 'Lie down with your feet up. No, let me,' he said, when she tried to pull her shoes off and performed the task for her. 'Just rest there until you feel better.'

Her eyes closed against the dizziness. Rachel opened her mouth to apologise and then closed it. It seemed there was one person in her life that neither needed nor wanted her apologies.

She had no idea how long she lay there, but eventually the spinning slowed enough to think. No, Armand had never needed her apologies from the first day.

She'd always known a crush on him was inevitable. But her feelings weren't based on his looks alone—though she'd never met a man more handsome—or his wealth, because he never flaunted it. It was just as he'd said to her: *I want you, only you.*

He expected nothing of her but for her to be who she was. He didn't want the Mrs Pete persona created by the Dr Pete phenomenon. He didn't want or need her to be the one to take the blame for him, because he was strong enough to accept his own consequences.

He just liked her. Just Rachel: no make-up, no glamorous clothing, no reed-thin figure or mahogany hair.

Her hand moved about until it found something warm, strong, human—his hand. She threaded her fingers through his, unable to talk, but suddenly her mind was clearer than it had ever been.

She was done—not just with apologising, but with accepting the criticisms levelled at her as fact for so long.

She turned her head, looking at him. He was crouched beside her, concern written all over his beautiful, intensely masculine face. She squeezed his hand and murmured, 'You really like me—just me?' She didn't mean to make it a question, but the habits of a lifetime took more than a lightning epiphany to change.

He nodded, a slow smile lighting his eyes, if not his mouth, warm and gentle—tender, almost. He murmured back, 'I like you…just you. And I want you. Just you.'

The little sigh seemed to come up from the deepest part of her heart. 'I need time to believe that, Armand. I need space.'

Those cloud-grey eyes were steady on hers, but without a hint of anger. 'Probably more than both of us knew.'

'Yes,' she sighed, and closed her eyes again.

'I think we should stay here a day or two,' he said quietly. 'Maman will be happy to put us up. She thinks you're wonderful.'

'I think she's wonderful too.' A little smile hovered around her mouth, but she didn't open her eyes.

'I think you're pretty wonderful too, Rachel,' he said softly. 'I've thought so from the hour we met.'

A lump formed in her throat and she couldn't answer—somehow even thanking him seemed fraught with dangerous belief. 'It's been a long day.'

'It's been a very long and hard day for you.' He pulled his hand from hers. She felt him rising, standing. 'Wait here a moment and don't think of anything.'

'Hmm,' she agreed, wishing she could stop

thinking. In her lifetime, her inability to turn off her busy brain had been her life's bane—again, more than Armand knew. 'I'm so glad you like me,' she whispered. 'I like you too.'

'Rachel?'

She started a little; she must have fallen asleep, or half-drifted there. 'Hmm?'

'Drink this. I think you'll like it.'

Again she felt herself lifted, cradled against him until she was on his lap, half-sitting upright. Breathing in, she caught a fragrant, spicy scent, piquant and fruity. She sipped at the glass at her lips and sighed in happy contentment at the warm sweetly-spiced wine. 'Ooh, this is delicious. What is it?'

'It's called *glühwein*. It basically means "glowing wine", because it's served warm in winter. Maman makes it every winter, and keeps a dozen bottles in the cellar. She finds it reviving to her spirits.'

'I know why your mother loves it,' she murmured when she'd almost emptied two glasses of it. 'I can't even remember what had me so upset before. I like your mother's wine, Armand. I like your mother. She's amazing.' She took a final sip, licking her lips to savour the final dregs. 'Hmm.

I like you too. Did I tell you I like you? I mean, really, I *like* you.' She smiled up at him, feeling all shiny and kind of fuzzy—like Armand's face right now. 'I do like you, and it's not just because you're so incredibly gorgeous, or because you feed me or give me airsick bags, or because you have the most gorgeous accent, or because you're a good kisser.'

'What is this "good kisser" rubbish? I'll have you know I'm a great kisser,' he retorted in mock indignation, but with a smile more tender than she'd ever seen before.

She giggled, finding it very funny. 'Well, not to challenge you, Armand, but I wouldn't really know.'

'Are you sure that's not another challenge?' he whispered in her ear. 'If it is, I wish you'd repeat it when you're not inebriated.'

She shivered with longing. 'Hmm.' She closed her eyes. 'Did I tell you how much I like it when you tease me and make me laugh even when I want to cry? I've never had so much fun before, Armand. I've never had a friend like you.'

'I thought you were enjoying my company, but thank you for telling me.' His lips brushed over her temple. She felt herself being lifted up into his arms. He was so strong, he never made her feel as if she was overweight... 'You need to sleep.'

She nestled into his shoulder and was asleep before he'd reached the top of the stairs leading to the bedrooms. Her last thought as she lay co-cooned in masculine warmth and strength was that she'd finally met a man strong enough to show when he cared, to tease her out of the blues and never betray her confidence. But there had to be a hitch somewhere.

No man could be this perfect. If he was, then she'd have to go, to leave him to find her own sphere, because she was far too imperfect to reach for the stars.

CHAPTER TEN

SUNLIGHT filtered through the slits in the window shutters, enough to wake Rachel from a deep sleep. She blinked and rubbed her eyes, taking a moment to reorient herself.

The room was a pretty one painted a soft pink, with sheer curtains around the four-poster bed. It was obviously a girl's room. The double bed only had dints where she'd lain, she noted with relief.

A soft knock sounded at the door, and she realised that was what had woken her. 'Come in,' she said, rubbing her eyes again. She felt muddle-headed, groggy.

The door opened and a timelessly lovely face with pixie-cut silver hair peeked around it. 'Good morning, Rachel, I hope you slept well?'

'Yes, thank you, Claire.' She smiled without effort. It was ridiculous to feel intimidated by a woman as kind and gentle as she was beautiful and famous.

'Would you like to join us for breakfast, or have it here on a tray?'

To her surprise she felt very hungry. 'I'll join you, thank you.'

Claire smiled with genuine happiness. 'I'm glad, as we didn't get to know each other very well last night. The bathroom is two doors down the hall to your right, with everything you'll need.' She closed the door behind her.

As soon as she came downstairs to the bright winter-garden room—a glass construction at the back of the house, rather like a hot house with a dining table in the centre of the flowers—Rachel sensed something wasn't right. Quickly, she looked at Armand, who was setting the table with bright napkins and cutlery with an odd expression on his face, as if he was rehearsing words. 'What is it? What's wrong?'

Still holding the silverware, he looked at her. She read the hesitation in his eyes before he seemed to come to his decision. 'I had a call from the resort an hour ago. Your husband checked in last night, demanding a room and demanding to see you.'

She felt the blood drain from her face even as she nodded. 'I'm only surprised it took him this long,' she said with a calmness that felt like the prelude to a storm, totally false. 'Excuse me for a minute.' She ran back up the stairs to her room, and pulled her mobile phone from her handbag. For the first time in weeks, she turned it on.

Feeling Armand's presence standing behind her ten seconds later rather than hearing it, she handed him the phone. 'He's left over two-hundred messages. I've exceeded my phone capacity, but read the last one he sent.'

'Can he contest the divorce? Have you given him any grounds?' was all he said after reading the message.

'I'm not sure. I've never been divorced before.' She tried to laugh.

'Has he grounds for this action?' Armand pressed. 'Have you given him any reason to contest it?'

She shook her head. 'This has to be a bluff to intimidate me. Then he'll come to me and try to charm me into coming back. He wants me to save his show and his ratings. That's all he cares about. But I don't know what's in his counter claim.' She frowned. 'I'll call my lawyer as soon as it turns office hours on the West Coast.'

'He said he'd left you for a younger woman.' He didn't quite make it a question. He stood about five feet from her; either he was giving her space to maintain her silence, or he was keeping his distance from the married woman.

No matter what his reasons were for keeping away, it was time. She either trusted him by now or she ran, and she was done with running. 'He did—after I changed the locks. But he was already seeing her at that point, he had been for a few months.'

'When did he break your arm?'

'The day I changed the locks,' she murmured, feeling the relief of telling him flood through her. 'When he broke my ribs the first time, it was sudden fury. It couldn't have been an accident, as he claimed, but I decided to forgive him.'

'Because you loved him?'

His tone was reserved, withholding judgment or emotion. But she lifted her chin and turned to face him. 'Yes, because I loved him. He made me his world and I felt safe there for a long time— and happy. The first time he hit me, I forgave him because I couldn't face losing him…and also losing everything we'd worked twelve years to accomplish. But the second time I couldn't keep forgiving him because I had nowhere else to go.'

'Your family?' he asked, after a small silence where the question pulsed unspoken.

She shrugged, in a basic self-defence mechanism. 'They love him and the lifestyle he's given them. And Mama's forgiven Daddy a hundred times. Not for beating, but for infidelity.'

As if he sensed her anguished wish to leave that subject alone, he slowly nodded. 'Is forgiveness an option this time?'

'No.' A single word, but filled with resolution. 'It's over.'

He smiled at her then, and it was like rainbow shades of joy coming after a long, dark rainy night. 'Let's go down to breakfast.'

Her fingers twisted around each other. 'Your mother…'

'She'll understand and want to help.' His smile faded, but when he spoke it wasn't what she expected. 'Women didn't press charges against their husbands back then. She had too much to lose—but she left him in the end.' His eyes turned cold, distant, but it wasn't aimed at her. 'He died a month later.'

Her humiliation fled in an instant. Her gaze flew to him, realising what he'd left unsaid, given the mysterious circumstances of his father's death. 'Oh, Armand…'

His eyes met hers, smoking dark with memory. 'My father sent us to boarding schools when I was twelve, the girls ten and eight—after I realised where Maman's bruises came from.'

Rachel opened her mouth and closed it, her mind racing. *That's why she quit acting until your father's death?* She didn't ask, didn't have to—the timeline was perfect. Every puzzle piece about this man who seemed anything but a wolf fit into place now.

She should have known. She'd thought he'd been talking about his sister when she'd challenged him to 'man up', but it had been his beloved mother he felt he'd failed to protect.

Her arms were around his waist before she knew she'd moved; her cheek lay against his heart. His chin rested on her hair as he held her. No movement, no words necessary. Empathy was best given in silence.

'I called Johanna and Carla,' he said quietly

after a long minute. 'I think it's time we talked to Maman about our father.'

Rachel gulped down the sudden rush of tears. 'That was very brave of you.'

He didn't answer that. 'They'll be here this afternoon. You can tell them anything about yourself, or nothing. We're all here for you, whatever you decide.'

Her throat ached and burned with gratitude, with wistfulness. 'You have a wonderful family, Armand. You're blessed.'

He lifted her chin. 'We are your family now, too, for as long as you need us.'

Even if she knew why he was doing this—he'd failed his family, and needed to save someone— she still wanted to cry. There was no pride that would fight this need, a need not for help or salvation but simply for someone to care. 'Thank you.'

'I've told Max to hold Rinaldi off as long as possible, until the family's here and you've worked out what the next move is.'

You've worked out *your* next move, he'd said. He wasn't taking control, only offering support. To him, she was no victim but a woman able to stand alone and make her own choices.

And that broke weeks of control. She went up on her tiptoes, her hand winding around his neck, pulling him down to her.

Their lips met. Such a simple thing, yet kissing Armand felt new and beautiful, like a sunlit pond, like drinking cool, sweet water after not knowing she'd been parched for years. He didn't pull her closer, since she was already against his heart; he didn't deepen the kiss, but he caressed her back and waist as they explored each other with the tentative discovery of a young child touching its first butterfly.

He knew, understood somehow, that she couldn't bear passion, not yet. Not until...

With a smothered gasp she moved back no more than an inch. 'Armand, I'm free,' she whispered, still holding him, her eyes huge as she realised the truth. 'He can come now for all I care. I can deal with him. I feel free of him at last.'

He didn't ask why, didn't joke or congratulate her, or even try to kiss her again. If anyone could understand the significance of her words, it was Armand. 'Breakfast must be getting cold. Shall we go down?'

Once more he gave her the dignity and sense of

control she so desperately needed, when she could so easily have fallen apart. She released him, put her hand in his and they walked down the stairs that way. Together.

'That's a fantastic idea, Rachel,' Armand's mother said a few hours later, her gaze dropping to the table. 'He's used to your being compliant, agreeing to everything he wants. He is also used to being the one in control in all matters. To face him this way will show him who you have become.' Her fingers tapped on the tabletop, and Rachel ached for the woman who hadn't stood up to her abuser until it was almost too late.

'But she can't face him alone!'

Sitting across from them at the dining table, Johanna frowned at her brother: a storm unleashed on a safe target. 'Pardon me, Armand, but when did this become your choice to make, or your judgment call on what she ought to do with her private life? Did she give you permission to become her conscience?'

'Johanna, Rachel is Armand's friend. He's merely worried, *tres cher.*'

Low and filled with loving reproof, Claire's voice

stopped Johanna with her mouth still half-open. Her eyes darkened and grew stormy, strengthening her resemblance to Armand. Then she sighed. 'You're right, Maman.' With a sense of strain, she smiled at her brother. 'Go on with what you were saying, Rachel.'

Rachel deliberately didn't look at Armand as she repeated, 'I need to face him alone, to show him this isn't because of anyone's influence on me. He thinks he can still manipulate me by love, by coercion and the fear of what others think. And if I show up with a support group, or even one—' she slanted a small, apologetic look at the man still holding her hand '—he won't have any reason to see the change in me. He'll deal with you, Armand, and not me.'

'Do you care what he thinks of you?' Armand's withdrawn tone in no way hid the anger, the fear. Fear for her.

Yet the apology in her eyes vanished. 'Everyone cares what others think of them, Armand, including you. As for Pete, perhaps I just care because I need him to see the woman I now am. If he doesn't, he'll never back down. He'll keep fighting the divorce.'

'He won't if you turn up with the police threatening to reinstate your restraining order—publicly this time!'

'He won't hurt me again, Armand,' she reassured him quietly. 'He won't have the courage to do that, not on my turf where he has no influence over anyone that sees us. If I choose the time and place, and he has to comply, it will weaken him. The meeting begins and ends with me. My choices. My way.'

'Did that work for you, Maman?' he snarled, swivelling to look at his mother in open challenge. 'If I recall, that was when our father packed us all away.'

Claire gaped for a moment. 'This is not about me, Armand, and this man is not your father.'

Claire was right, yet a cold knot of fear hit Rachel in the stomach and took up residence. Turning to Armand again, she took both his hands in hers. 'I know Pete. You don't.'

'I can't let you meet him alone,' he muttered beneath his breath. 'If he hurts you…'

The words touched her somewhere deep inside, a place she hadn't known existed, because until now nobody had ever fought to protect her. 'I'll meet him in a public restaurant, where you can be waiting nearby,' she said gently. Finally she accepted that compromise was possible for her, because someone really cared about her welfare.

'I want to be there. Someone has to protect you from him,' he protested, as if hearing her thoughts.

'I know you want to protect me.' Still holding his hands, she looked up at him, and suddenly it was as if only the two of them existed in the room. 'But I need you to respect my decision, Armand. For me, and my future. For my self-respect and well-being. For my healing, I need to have control of this.'

'I hate this.' With a low growl, he released her hands and paced around the table. Watching him, she noticed for the first time that the other women had discreetly vanished.

'I know,' she said, understanding because it would be how she'd feel. 'But this has to be my decision, my way. I have to face him with my own strength, not yours.'

He swore for the first time in her hearing, stalking from one end of the room to the other and back again. 'I don't know why you doubt your strength, when you've been pushing me from the first day.'

'I only had the courage for that because I knew you'd never hurt me.' She stood in his path, blocking his incessant pacing. 'Armand, you've given me a priceless gift these past weeks: faith in myself, finding my own strength. Don't ever think I don't appreciate it. But it's time I used those gifts now.'

She spoke with finality and, though he gave that harsh sigh and swore again, he gave the barest nod before walking around her and out the back door, vanishing into the brilliant late-autumn day, a spectre of perfection she'd found and lost.

Rachel watched him leave, aching to follow, but he needed time. He wouldn't let go of his fierce protective instincts—if he hadn't been born with them, his family experiences had cemented them inside his soul—but he had to accept his limits, with her or with any woman. If he didn't do it now, he'd probably burst into the meeting with Pete with sword drawn.

Where they would go later, when the intensity of this situation was done and he didn't have to be her knight any more, she didn't know. When he realised she could stand alone, she'd probably have her heart dented, maybe even broken. Men like Armand only came along once in a lifetime, a true knight in shining armour. A man who was everything she'd ever dreamed of but believed didn't exist outside of fairy tales.

'He almost killed Papa, you know. When Maman left and took us out of school, and Armand came from the set of his second movie to visit, Papa found us. Armand was seventeen then. When Papa tried to force Maman to come with him, Armand broke his nose and arm.'

Unsurprised by Johanna's presence behind her, she nodded. 'I thought he might have done something like that.'

'You're good for Armand,' Johanna said softly. 'He's stopped being the perfect gentleman and has become the Wolf with you. It's a really good sign.'

'The Wolf?' Forgetting all about her insecurities about the beautiful women he'd dated, Rachel spun around to face Armand's sister, burning with curiosity.

Johanna smiled with a touch of sadness. 'He's not the lone wolf he's been painted to be. I nicknamed him the Wolf years ago because he's so protective and faithful—he never leaves the people he loves in need of anything. As for all the women he's been with, he was kind and gentle with them, but never the Wolf. You see, wolves only mate once, and it's for ever. When he truly loves a woman, it will be for life.' The look Johanna gave her made a treacherous warmth bloom in her heart, its tender petals breaking open through her entire body.

'Oh,' was all she could think to say, in wonder. *And he's the Wolf with me...?* But she couldn't bring herself to ask it. She was almost afraid of the answer.

'Did he tell you about our father, and why he sent us to boarding schools?'

Dumbly, she shook her head, suddenly aware that there was much more to this story than she had first imagined. 'We'd rather be here to tell her, Johanna.'

Johanna stared at her mother and Carla as they entered the room, but Claire's hand landed on Rachel's shoulder. 'It's time, and Rachel is the person. Come, sit down, *cher.* Armand will be back soon enough, and we all need to say this, to be united before he joins in. He needs to see us strong—for, though you were both hurt, Armand was the one the most deeply injured.'

Rachel is the person. What had Claire meant by that?

Armand's youngest sister Carla started the conversation in a slow, halting voice. 'I think I was about eight when my father first hit me. He said it wasn't a female's place to argue with the man of the house.'

'Tell her why he hit you,' Claire murmured with an arm around her daughter. 'It's time we all talked of this. I should have made us all do it long ago.'

The lids of Carla's eyes, the sky-blue of her mother's, dropped. 'I woke up, needing water, and I saw him hit Maman. She was crying. I cried too. I told him he was hurting her, to stop it. So he—he backhanded me across the face.'

'You never told me!' Johanna cried.

Carla sighed. 'After Maman calmed me down, he put me to bed. He kissed me and said it never happened, that I had a bad dream...'

'And I told her the same the next day, when she asked me about it.' Claire nuzzled Carla's hair in loving apology. 'I wanted her to forget it, put it out of her mind. I didn't want her as damaged as I'd become.'

'He hit me twice,' Johanna mumbled. 'The second time, Maman left him. He said I was defiant.'

Claire nodded. 'I knew it would never end then,' she said, softly, sadly.

'And Armand?' Johanna asked, frowning. 'What did you tell Armand after he stopped him hitting you that time and he sent us all away?'

Claire looked down, her hands trembling. 'Your father never hit me again after that until after I left him, Johanna, nor did he hit Carla. I think Armand knocking him down shocked him. But he wasn't strong enough to stand your defiance without lashing back.'

'How often did he hit you?' Rachel asked, because Johanna couldn't bear to ask it, couldn't bear to not know.

'Not as much as you think, *chérie*,' Claire said to her oldest daughter, sitting like stone across the table. 'Most of the time he was a loving husband. But when things got stressful with work, if he drank too much or if he lost money and I said or did something to upset him…'

Rachel took Claire's hand in hers. 'You know that's not the truth, Claire. Weak people blame others for their mistakes and faults. Abusers never take responsibility until they've received help.'

Claire looked down. 'That is why I said you're the person to hear our stupid story, Rachel. Not because of your degree, but because of your experience and your empathy. But don't waste it on me—I have come to terms with the past.'

'Just not enough to talk to your children about it,' she said softly. 'I am not the person, Claire, because I clearly still have my own issues to fix. You're the one your children need to hear this from. Talk to them—talk to Johanna and Carla while I find Armand. And then talk to him too.' She touched the older woman's arm as she was trying to shake her head. 'You're too strong to let yourself off the hook, Claire. Talk to them. And I'll find Armand.'

CHAPTER ELEVEN

ARMAND was walking back from the wild edge of the village, where the road led to the next town, when Rachel found him. By the abrupt stride and the preoccupied frown, he had yet to find peace about her decision, and he had more pain yet to come.

Aching for him, she waited for him to reach her. 'Hi.'

How lame was that, Rachel?

'Hi.' Now the intense look turned on her. 'Did you need to find me for some reason?'

That's Armand, she thought, a touch of tenderness shooting through her despite the unnerving expression he wore. *Straight to the point, needing a battle to concentrate on.*

When she hesitated, his eyes darkened. 'Is it Rinaldi? Does he know where you are?'

'No. Not yet, but I'll call him soon.' She reached out to him, twined her fingers through his as she tried to find the right words. 'Johanna told me about how you stopped your father from hitting your mother.'

His jaw tightened. 'Too little too late,' he muttered, pulling his hand away. 'Are you worried I'll hit Rinaldi now?'

Although she bit her lip, the smile came through the repressed cheek. 'More like reassured, Armand. You're bigger than he is.'

The chuckle was reluctant. 'So I can hover nearby, just in case?' he asked with something approaching sarcasm. It told her more than she wanted to know.

She crossed her arms beneath her breasts and tried not to glare at him, but she was unable to stop the hurt from showing in her eyes. 'You really don't think I can handle him, do you?'

'Don't make this personal, Rachel. He broke your ribs, your wrist!'

She turned from the anger so clearly written all over his face, the protectiveness he refused to control. 'Yes, he did. And I handled it.'

'By running halfway across the world,' he shot back. 'You didn't even press charges.'

'I lodged the x-rays with my lawyer,' she

said quietly. 'I needed time. Until I came to Switzerland, he was all I had. Everything and everyone else believed in him.'

'And now?'

The challenge in his tone was almost insulting, but with a strong effort she managed to hang onto her temper. 'Now I will do what I must to end his belief that I'll tolerate any more manipulation or abuse. But you need to think of your family.'

Like a shot he changed, moving around her to see her face, fierce concern in every line of him. 'Why, what's wrong?'

Gently now, she said, 'Your mother has things to tell you that all of you need to hear. She's waiting for you.'

He did that statue thing again, freezing in place. 'I don't want to hear it.'

'I know,' she whispered, closing her eyes, taking a step closer. Right now touching him was the last thing he wanted, and a risk she had to take. He jerked back when she caressed his face, but she opened her eyes, took another step and touched him again. 'But sometimes what we want isn't what we need the most. What we want doesn't help our loved ones. And sometimes what we fear the most isn't the worst thing we can go through.'

Armand swore savagely, pushing her off. 'Stop pushing me, Rachel. I said no.'

'So did I to your arguments, and yet I know you're right.' It hurt her physically to admit the truth, but it had to be said, for his sake as well as her own. 'Though part of me wants to face Pete totally alone and know I'm strong enough to do it without help, what I need is to know you're near me, just in case.'

He threw her a look brimming with suspicion. 'Why do I get the feeling that you just handed me a consolation prize?'

Her mouth twisted sideways in a rueful half-smile. 'Probably because you know that I want something in return. I want you to help your mother heal, and your sisters.'

He whitened. 'Damn you, Rachel,' he muttered in repressed fury. '*Damn* you.'

She watched him stride towards the house, tears stinging her eyes. The memory of the pain burning in his betrayed eyes would haunt her long after he'd forced himself to give his family what they needed.

Would the cost of the Bollinger family truth session be the fledgling trust between them? Had the Armand and Rachel story just become another blip in the life and times of the Wolf, not even worthy of an item in the news? Had it ended before it had truly begun?

It was almost two hours before Armand came out the same way he'd walked in—but either the world had changed or he wasn't the same man.

Though his life just might or might not have fallen to pieces, he could still look up and see the sunshine over the snow-capped peaks of the French Alps. He could breathe in and smell the scent of fallen leaves and drying grass.

And he could still smile at the sight of the wise, beautiful, strong-willed and temporary intrusion into his life hopping from foot to foot, clearly in pain, and in more than anxiety over his family session. 'Everything okay?' The worry in her voice was reflected in her eyes as she searched his face.

'Everything's fine, Rachel. Now, get to the bathroom before you explode,' he said, hiding the grin, not knowing yet if she deserved to have that reprieve.

With a swift, nervous look and bitten lip, she bolted into the house but, just as she'd done last night, she stopped politely when Maman called her. He watched through the window, an outsider, as his mother and sisters all hugged her and she hugged them back, looking the same yet somehow more peaceful.

Then she turned her face and gave him a swift, uncertain smile, including him even though he'd punished her.

He'd punished her for giving his family closure and serenity. The only cost was to the denial that had been his one self-indulgence, but it had hurt the people he loved most.

Once, he'd believed he'd done all he could to protect them, to make them happy and safe. Once upon a time—until Rachel had walked into his cabin, invaded every secret he'd thought well hidden from the world and showed him he'd done everything but the one thing they needed most: to listen, to heal them.

No wonder you brought her to me. She's special, Armand.

He waited until she'd run upstairs before coming back in. He wasn't ready for a group-hug session that included her. Right now he needed space from all these new emotions churning through him, and he needed time to work out what they were.

Right now only one stood out clearly: *I should never have kissed her.* He'd taken their friendship into a realm that neither of them was ready to explore.

Was it too late to go back?

Then he got the call that changed the direction of his thoughts entirely.

'Please leave me alone with Rachel,' he said to his family in a tone of courteous command when he'd disconnected, and they quietly vanished.

When Rachel came back down, he said baldly, 'He's worked out where we are from an interview he read about Maman. He's on his way here.'

He saw the colour drain from her face.

Despite her efforts at self-control, Rachel felt herself sway. 'Is it possible for an American citizen to take out a restraining order here?'

After a few moments, Armand said slowly, 'Since he's on his way here, I'd say no. I am certain he'd check on that law before he flew over.'

'That sounds like Pete. He wouldn't risk wrecking his career if it got out,' she replied with soft bitterness. 'Yes, you're right—and the temporary one I took out has lapsed.'

Armand took a step towards her and, after a hesitation, enfolded her in his arms, breathing together, just breathing, for a few precious moments. It was her turn to receive that empathy unspoken. 'So what do you want to do now?' he asked eventually.

'If I know him, he's sitting smugly in some aircraft, thinking I'm going to go back with him after a few nice words and kisses. And if that doesn't work...' She fingered her wrist for a moment before she pulled back to look up at Armand's face, tender and troubled.

His obvious concern steeled her spine.

'It's time to take control now, before he sees me.'

Before she could change her mind, she dialled the number of the man who'd once been her world.

Rachel was sitting in the restaurant alone when Pete walked in two hours later.

She watched Pete wind his way towards her, tall and well-built, so handsome and perfectly groomed. The movie-star quality he'd always had shone so brightly it lit the room. And he was smiling at her in the way that had never failed to make her want to do anything for him.

Watching him, she marvelled that his perfect face no longer made her insides flip. How had she never noticed the touch of sulkiness before, the charm that had such a spoiled-brat quality to it?

Or perhaps he was sulky now because she'd out-manoeuvred him even in this small matter. No doubt he'd expected to show up, stun her, smile at her and win her back.

Rachel lifted her chin, her mind racing. The plan was complete. She sat at the table in the centre of the restaurant where everyone could see them. Public opinion was everything to Pete; he'd do nothing to her here, where everyone could have a phone camera and Internet connection. He'd play the 'wooing lover' card, counting on her being lonely by now, and if that didn't work she knew he'd try to blackmail her somehow.

Despite her nerves, she had to hold in a smile. Pete didn't know what he was in for. A dozen other tables were taken—four of them by Bollinger family friends. Armand's sisters sat two tables away, pretending to chat as they drank too much coffee. Armand waited in the side room, where he could see them, but Pete couldn't see him. Because her famous face could alert Pete, Claire had elected to stay at home, but was anxiously waiting for news.

She wasn't alone—and that made all the difference.

'Hi, bunny. You look beautiful,' Pete said softly when he reached the table. He made no mention of her weight, hair colour or lack of extensions. 'But you always look beautiful to me.'

Yes, he was playing the Prince Charming card. What a shame for him that she'd met the real thing.

'The name's Rachel,' she said coolly. 'Please, sit down.'

'I love this place. Very rustic, ye olde world charm with all the carved tables and chairs and the ceiling beams. It's so fifteenth-century. No wonder you like it.' He came around the table, leaning in to kiss her.

Rachel kept her face stony without a hint of welcome. She didn't turn her face from him—he'd take it as fear of her reaction to him—but she didn't accept the kiss, no matter how he lingered on her lips. She counted three before she slowly moved back. 'I said, sit down.'

With a smile that seemed fixed, Pete caressed her shoulder for a few moments. *I'm the one in control*, his look said, even though the look of love was dominant. He had a plan—seduce her, make her want to come back—and he'd stick to it.

Pete never had a Plan B. He always had to win on his terms and, until today, she hadn't known it for the weakness it was.

'I knew you wouldn't abandon your T-shirts,' he said softly, allowing his fingers to trail over her shoulder before he finally moved to sit opposite her. He pointed at the shirt she wore. It was one of her favourites. 'It's how I found you. My PI took a shot of you standing outside your...cabin, wearing one. You looked just like the girl I met twelve years ago.'

She said nothing in reply. Anything she said now he'd take as capitulation.

'Did you order for us?' he asked, managing to make the question sound intimate.

She called over the waiter with a hand motion. 'This gentleman wishes to order,' she said in French.

The waiter asked Pete in French what he'd like. Pete frowned at Rachel. 'You know I don't speak French. Why don't you order for me, bunny? You know what I like.'

Once upon a time that tone would have melted her—but she wasn't that woman now, dependent on his affection. She smiled at the waiter. 'This gentleman doesn't speak French—do you speak English?'

The waiter handed Pete an English menu. 'What would you like, sir?' he asked in flawless English.

Rachel watched as Pete struggled with his temper. He'd always hated being at a disadvantage with anyone. Being faced with two people more knowledgeable than him at one time was too much for him to handle with equanimity. 'What are you having, bunny?' Pete asked at last, his gaze touching hers over the rim of the menu.

She handed the closed menu back to the waiter with another smile. 'Nothing for me, thank you. My *name*,' she enunciated with a distinct lack of warmth, 'Is Rachel.'

He tilted his head a little with a puzzled smile. So charming—yet she couldn't understand how she'd once been so charmed by it. 'You always loved being my bunny.'

She wasn't about to be drawn into a discussion of the past. 'Why are you contesting the divorce? What are your grounds?'

A flush touched his cheeks; his eyes flashed to the waiter and his jaw worked. 'I'll have a coffee to start, thanks,' he said briefly, handing back his menu. When he'd gone, Pete said coolly, 'It seems to me you've lost your manners, speaking so in front of a stranger.'

Instead of feeling chastened, she grinned. 'Only with people I feel no need to impress. My friends here think I have wonderful manners.'

His face darkened for a moment. He hated her having friends or anyone in her life that didn't have his loyalties at heart first—and the reference to not caring if she impressed him had got to him. 'Well, your family don't agree. When was the last time you called them?'

She blinked, and if the smile felt forced she accepted it. She knew her family would always have the power to wound her—especially because her family loved her enemy more than her. 'I believe just after you called and asked them to guilt-trip me into returning, or at least into discovering where I was,' she replied bluntly.

She watched his cheeks darken with colour and his jaw tighten before he remembered he needed to charm her. 'They love you, bunny. They want you to come home.'

'You mean they want me back on the show that gave them money and prestige,' she retorted. 'They love you. To them, I'm just the smart freak that got famous by accident.'

His jaw dropped a little at her blunt, accurate assessment of her family's feelings for her. 'Rachel, how dare…?' Then he seemed again to remember: *charm her.* 'I think you need to remember your own words on the show, bunny: *forgiveness is the key to finding peace, and the ability to move on.* They do love you. They just didn't know what to do with you all those years until I came along.' And his eyes filled with smugness for a moment before, again, he returned to his loving look.

Rachel frowned, watching his face change over and over, and realised his expressions were like masks he could take on and off at will.

The same masks he'd always used on her to get his way.

But now her blinders were gone. He didn't love her; he probably never had. He loved himself far too much and deeply to have room for anyone else—and all she felt was relief that, in walking away, she wouldn't hurt anything but his ego.

Funny; she'd thought the feeling of power, of controlling the situation, would be heady, or at least a good novelty, but instead she felt a twinge of pity for him. Fame and power was such a sad substitute for real happiness. And he didn't even know it.

So she dropped the game. 'Pete, I don't really care what pretext you used to stall the divorce. I want the divorce—from you, and from the show.'

He stilled with his hand halfway towards the water glass the waiter had brought him. 'And if I say I don't want it? What if I want you back, bunny—in my life and the show?'

She met his loving, pleading look squarely. 'You and I both know you wouldn't be here but for the ratings drop, and the offer I received—but that's not the issue. I don't want you, Pete. Not in any way.'

'So it's true,' he said very quietly, yet with the lightning change to venomous fury that used to make her shudder. 'You want your own show—after I *made* you.'

She didn't bother retaliating. People with self-delusions rarely let go of them. She knew she'd made him, and made the show, with her knowledge—and that was enough. 'I want the divorce. Make it happen—withdraw your counter claim.'

He lifted a brow, jutted his jaw. 'Or you'll do what?'

'Do you really need me to answer that?' She rubbed her wrist, and watched him whiten with the unspoken threat. 'I have the x-rays and copies of the restraining order lodged with three separate lawyers I've never used before. You can't reach them.'

He opened his mouth and closed it. His eyes moved as his mind raced, working out how to answer that.

Again she found herself taking pity on him. 'I can destroy you, but for the sake of all those years together I'd prefer not to. This divorce is happening no matter what, so let's make it as amicable as we can.'

'I told you I never meant to hurt you. You're my life, Rachel. Can't you forgive me and get past it?'

His tone was pleading, the wooing lover again; his hands reached out to hers.

His wedding ring was firmly in place. *Nice touch*, she thought, and almost laughed.

Her hands remained on her lap as she gave up trying to use reason and went for the jugular. 'So the producers won't renew the show's contract without me on board, is that it?'

Abandoning the act faster than she could have hoped for, his face relaxed into naked anger and he nodded curtly. 'You know they won't—they want the double act or nothing. Carol has already told you, no doubt.'

He couldn't know that Rachel hadn't bothered to open any of her agent's texts yet. She'd wanted this situation sorted before she even considered the TV deal.

And it was then, only then, she realised she'd thought of Carol's texts before remembering what Pete had admitted—that he was only here for the show—and marvelled that it didn't hurt at all.

Scraping the chair back, she stood, all five-foot-one of her in her jeans and running shoes. 'It's over, Pete—the show and the marriage. Let the divorce go through, or I'll be forced to measures

I don't want to take. But be assured I will—doctors' testimony, x-rays and all.'

He glanced around the room to see who had heard before he answered, low and hard with real venom. 'I should have known coming here wouldn't be worth it. Go, then, have your damned divorce, go back to your new man. You won't last a month with Bollinger—he's a serial philanderer, even with really beautiful women. You'll come crawling back after he's ditched you, and I'll laugh. I don't need you, anyway! I'll make it without you—I'll do better. I'll hit the Top Five in chat shows! See if I don't.'

'I hope you do,' she said sincerely.

He shot her a glance of loathing and walked out with careful dignity, smiling and nodding at everyone he passed, showing the world who'd won.

When he was gone, she released the breath she didn't know she'd been holding, whispered, 'I'm free,' and laughed and laughed. And she kept laughing when Carla and Johanna came to her and put their arms around her in celebration. They jumped together like cheerleaders in a victory dance, while the other restaurant patrons pretended nothing was happening, as they'd been instructed.

'Can I join in the fun?' Armand's amused and relieved tone came from behind her—and without stopping to think about it she turned and jumped into his open arms.

CHAPTER TWELVE

RACHEL jumped into Armand's waiting arms and his sisters, smiling, moved back to the table to wait.

'It's finally over, Armand,' she murmured, hugging him tight. 'I'm free at last.'

'You did it.' His arms closed around her, and he swung her around in circles until they were outside on the balcony overlooking the valley. 'You're free, Rachel, and you did it alone.'

'I really did. I can't quite believe it yet. It's like I've just woken up from a dream.' She hugged him again. 'He's gone, Armand. He's *gone*.'

He laughed and nodded, his forehead brushing her hair. 'Like bubonic plague. You swept that old rat's flea out of here.'

She burst out laughing at the analogy. 'I kind of pity him, you know? It's like control and success is all he has. Without it, he's nothing.'

He didn't look too compassionate as he said,

'Well, you might have started him on the road to reality, but now he can't ride back to fame on your coat tails.'

A massive smile filled her heart and radiated from her face. 'You really think so?'

'That makes a difference to you?' he asked, but it was a little too careless.

Why the question surprised her so much, she didn't know. That he cared for her was miracle enough—and he'd shown her too many times now for her to doubt it—but this…

Was he jealous?

Suddenly she was aware that this was the closest they'd ever been without a snowboard, a sled or any other pretext for touching. They were meshed together so tight she could feel his heart thumping hard against her chest, and she knew how worried he'd been for her.

I want you, only you.

Still hardly daring to believe in what her years of training told her must be true, she murmured, 'I'm a psychologist, Armand. It's what I've been trained to do, to read people, to heal people. But I'd failed with him for so long, I'd begun to think the problems had to be mine.'

With a low, growling sound almost of fury, he muttered, 'His problems were never your fault. You know about projection—how some people push the blame for their weaknesses onto the nearest object who'll accept it—but you don't apply it to those around you. When are you going to wake up, Rachel?' He hauled her up so they were equal, then he turned her face to his. 'You're free of him now. You said it.' And he kissed her, deep, hard and possessively.

For the first time he wasn't gentle with her, but she realised he knew what she hadn't known. That freedom had come, the choice to give him her passion or not, and she must have been looking at him with all the yearning in her body and heart.

And then her mind, heart and body were filled to overflowing, not just with passion and demand, but her own driving need for him. Her arms and lips were filled with Armand, and she loved it. The late autumn sun came out in sudden brilliance, shining on her back as she melted into him. Like a snowman in sunshine, she was melting in a kiss—something she'd believed only happened in the movies. Her arms were around his neck so tight she must have been cutting off his breathing, but he merely growled and heaved her even closer against him so there was nothing but beating hearts, uneven breathing and this deep, passionate kiss. This wonderful, perfect kiss that made a woman of her, a kiss that taught her the difference between existing and truly living. This kiss taught her the difference between a lonely girl's adoration of her rescuer, and a woman's lasting love, because it was Armand kissing her. Because it would probably always be Armand for her now…and knowing that didn't even frighten her any more.

Minutes or hours passed while they kissed; she didn't know or care, this glorious moment was all she craved. Then he trailed his lips over her face, murmuring endearments in French, and she was completely gone. 'Armand, oh Armand, I want you.' She turned her face, found his mouth with hers, and another brief eternity winged silently past as they stood locked together, totally absorbed in what was, to her, the kiss of a lifetime.

Much later, her face buried in his shoulder, she whispered, shaken, 'You were right.'

'Of course I was. About what?' he chuckled into her hair, kissing her temple.

'You are a *great* kisser.'

'Oui?' he murmured into her ear, lifting her chin. His smile was beautiful, honest and open, and it melted her anew. 'More?'

Her entire body was turning into a mess of heated honey pooling at his feet. 'Oh yes, yes, Armand… I want more, much more. I…' She kissed him, slow and lingering, while she gathered courage from his dark groan and his aroused body's rough movement against her. 'I want to drag you to the nearest bed and not leave it for a week.'

He drew in a breath. 'And you had to tell me this now, when we're staying with my mother and sisters, not when we had the cabin to ourselves?'

Still a foot off the ground, she wound her hand through his hair and laughed, soft and rippling. 'I didn't know you were such a great kisser then.'

'Nor were you ready to know. And I did not know that you were capable of doing this to me, either, though I'd suspected it wasn't going to be like it was before.' He kissed her ear and she shivered with the power of his simplest touch. 'I have a feeling a week won't be enough. A month at least.'

A whole month of making love with Armand…

Just thinking about it brought on another shiver. What was he *doing* to her? 'Maybe two months,' she dared to venture between kisses as heated as they were tender.

'Three or four,' he muttered, and groaned as she kissed his throat in near-shocked joy that he wanted her so badly. 'No. If you come to my bed, Rachel, don't plan on leaving that bed for at least a year. I'll stop you any way I can.'

A year with Armand. It was more than she'd dared to hope for. Another soft, lingering kiss near the base of his throat, where his pulse beat madly. Then she looked up and her eyes twinkled. 'I think we might have killed poor Frau Heffernan by that point.'

He chuckled between lingering kisses on her nose, eyes and mouth. 'They'd find her frozen on the *terrasse.*'

'She can be the new Ice Man. They'll call her the Peeking Woman.'

He looked into her eyes. 'I call you beautiful.'

She couldn't turn away when he looked at her like that; she *felt* beautiful and desired. With a will of its own, her hand slipped inside his jacket. She caressed his back through his thick shirt, and even touching him that much made a little strangled sound emerge from her throat. 'Armand, I want you so much it hurts.'

His eyes darkened with slumbering fire. 'We could fly home today. Or we could drive to an excellent bed and breakfast run by a friend of mine on this side of the Alps where we'd be totally spoiled without leaving the bed. Or I have a chalet an hour away that's totally private, with its own spa and sauna. It's fully stocked, and we can cook for ourselves.' His kiss left her in a mess of hot shivers. 'Your wish is my command.'

Now she understood the flash in his eyes when she'd said those words to him on their first week together. There was something almost unbearably sensual in hearing them, evoking images. 'Which one is closest?' she whispered urgently. 'How soon can we leave?'

Another kiss, rough and desperate with need. Then, holding her so tight she couldn't tell whether she felt her own heart beating or his, he muttered, 'We need to thank Maman and the girls. I need to say goodbye to my nieces and nephew.'

Something flattened inside her. 'Oh…of course, I'm sorry. I'm being so rude, after all they did…'

'Shh.' He laid a finger on her lips. 'No more apologies, remember? My family doesn't need them. I don't need them, either. I need you, just as you are.'

She felt her lips fall apart. 'Oh, Armand, what a *wonderful* thing to say.'

He nuzzled her mouth. 'I want this as much as you do. We'll be alone tonight.'

There were so many things she wanted to say, none of them appropriate. The end would come in its time. When he finished it and wanted to move on, she'd smile and not beg him to stay. But now was the beginning filled with wonders and possibilities. So she buried her face in his throat for a moment, just breathing him in, before wriggling a bit. 'Then let me down and don't touch me until we're alone again. I've got almost no hope of not embarrassing us both in front of your family as it is, but if you touch me...'

He let her feet touch the floor but, breaking her command immediately, he tipped up her face. When she met his gaze, the tenderness in his eyes melted her anew and made her forget everything but him. 'They already know about us, *mon doux*.

Even if they hadn't seen the way I look at you, they'd know simply because I—'

Her phone buzzed at that moment. Agonised, she whispered, 'I'm sorry, I'll switch it off.' Then she looked at the caller and frowned. 'No, wait, it's my mother. If I don't take it, she'll just keep calling.'

'Family, eh?' He kissed her nose. 'Take it, *mon doux*.'

My sweet. The words almost made her switch the phone off again. But something made her hit the 'accept' button. 'Hi, Mama, how are you... *What?*' Within seconds she swayed where she stood. 'When?' she asked dully. 'I—I'm so sorry, Mama. I know, I'm so sorry...'

At first angered that her mother seemed to be demanding apologies within seconds of talking to her daughter for the first time in months, Armand saw the whiteness of Rachel's face, her eyes shining with tears about to spill over, felt her whole body shaking, and knew something was seriously wrong. He wrapped his arm around her shoulders, held her close and waited for her to tell him.

'I'll be home on the first available flight,' she murmured unsteadily. 'I know. I love you too,

Mama.' She disconnected the call and looked up at him with the expression of a shot fawn. 'Daddy passed away ten minutes ago in the hospital. He— had a heart attack. He'd been sick for a week, but nobody knew where I was, and because I didn't check email and I had my—my stupid phone switched off, I wasn't there. *I wasn't there.*'

A few minutes before, Armand had noted that his friend Patric had closed the balcony curtains. He was even more grateful for it now as he drew her into both his arms and let her cry out her first grief. He'd been where she was now, and knew she'd later hate it if anyone but he had seen her weeping. 'Ah, *mon doux, mon chérie,*' he whispered, holding her against his heart and aching for her. 'I know,' he murmured, rocking her slowly while her body jerked with the force of her choked tears. 'I know. I'm here.'

'But I c-couldn't say that,' she whispered, muffled against his shirt. His shirt was wet with her tears, a gift of her trust. 'I w-wasn't there, Armand. I should have checked my phone. W-why didn't I check m-my *stupid phone*?'

Why hadn't I been there to stop him? It was the question he'd been asking himself for eighteen years. Had his father died accidentally in that fire, or had he killed himself in shame for abusing his family? He'd asked that too for years without an answer, without healing. 'You thought you had good reason, *chérie.*'

She shook her head violently. 'Y-you know the w-worst thing? Pete was here. He knew how sick Daddy was and he d-didn't even tell me...'

He wasn't going to touch that; telling her he wanted to kill Rinaldi wouldn't help her now, only misdirect her grief into anger and blame that wouldn't help her get through this traumatic time. But if he saw Rinaldi at her mother's house, he'd take him outside and teach him to try bullying a *man.*

Control it. Think of Rachel. 'You'll be with your family by tonight, US time. I'll take you.'

'W-what?' Her eyes, drowned in tears, gazed up at him in wonder. 'You... You'd really do that f-for me?'

If he hadn't been almost sure before, looking into those beautiful drenched eyes that said, *'you're my prince, my hero'* did it. He'd never forget that look—and he'd never forget the moment he knew he was in love for the first and last time in his life. The Wolf had finally found his mate, when and where he'd least expected it—and he'd never felt so exhilarated or so terrified. 'Of course.' It was all he could say because everything else was entirely inappropriate, given her sadness.

'B-but… My fam— My mama…' Tears filled her eyes anew as she amended 'my family'. 'At home, at the…*funeral*,' she added, trying to sound strong. 'Mama will—will punish you for not being Pete, for being an outsider.' She sniffed again. 'Knowing Pete, he's running the whole thing like the show. He'll take centre stage. Can you handle it?'

He almost melted with tenderness. Without meaning to, she'd told him she wanted him beside her when she faced her hardest moments. If she needed him there, he'd be there. 'I can handle your mother and Rinaldi, Rachel. Don't worry.' With all the love filling him, he kissed her lips so gently, almost afraid of breaking her. 'I am considered rather charming in certain circles, you know.'

It was watery, filled with heart-wrenching sadness, but she managed a tiny chuckle. 'Yes, I—I've felt that once or twice.' Then she melted back into his arms, sobbing quietly, and he held her in aching silence, empathy and love that must remain unspoken—for now or for ever, right now he didn't know.

His entire life had been founded on one certainty: he'd always be alone. Protecting his family, being there for them and recreating everything his father had lost, had been a full-time preoccupation for so long. The fear that one day, when he was pushed too far, he'd end up like his father had sealed the deal. He'd never marry. But Rachel was a 'for ever' woman, and he'd never take that lifetime of security from her.

He didn't know what the future held, if he could even be the man Rachel deserved—or even if she could ever love him.

'When can we leave?' she whispered, startling him out of his reverie.

'We'll be on our way within three hours. All we need to do is book the jet and they'll do the rest.' He kissed her hair. 'Maman will want to see you to console you. Do you wish this from her? If not, I can call her.'

'It's all right. I'm okay now,' she whispered unsteadily, trying so hard to pull away from him, to stand alone. 'Let's go see her. I need to thank her for everything.'

But she trembled and against her will her body swayed. 'You're in shock, Rachel.' He lifted her into his arms, and made a heroic effort not to think of what could have been this night. 'Let me do this for you, *mon doux*. Let me help you.'

Like she'd done last night, she dropped her head onto his shoulder and sighed. 'You're too good to me.'

'You make it easy,' he whispered, pushing open the balcony door.

'I don't understand why.' She sounded plaintive, but also halfway towards sleep.

'I know, but one day you will,' he whispered. He walked inside the restaurant and saw the smiles vanish from his sisters' faces at the sight of Rachel in his arms.

'But what will I do when you have to leave me? I know you will one day.'

She'd said it so softly he wasn't quite sure he had heard the correct words, especially after the exquisite half-hour they'd had on the balcony. 'Why do you think I want to leave you?'

She didn't answer.

He looked down at her. Her lashes had fluttered shut, either from embarrassment or sheer exhaustion, but she was still hiccupping as she breathed. Her face was flushed with drying tear-tracks down both cheeks.

She'd had one hell of a day.

He looked up and saw the worried faces of both his sisters right in front of him. 'What happened, Armand?' Johanna demanded, pale and shaken, assuming the worst.

'Has there been bad news?' Carla asked, frowning at Rachel with obvious concern.

'The worst news,' he said very quietly, trying not to relive the smug look on Rinaldi's face as he left the restaurant, knowing Rachel's jubilation would very soon turn to grief. 'I'll tell you at Maman's. Let's get her home where she can rest.'

CHAPTER THIRTEEN

IT WASN'T quite how he'd imagined waking up beside Rachel for the first time.

When the captain announced they were ninety minutes from landing at Austin, Armand woke in the enormous double seats they'd turned into a bed by lifting up the mutual arm-rest. Rachel hadn't been sick this time—that was what ordering the best possible jet could do—but she was exhausted, lying in his arms beneath a thin pile of blankets, her head on his chest, her breathing deep and even. But they were both fully dressed and she was still pale, with dark smudges beneath her eyes.

She'd woken a few times during the night, and he'd held her while she'd wept.

'You know the saddest part? I never really knew him, Armand. He was my father, but he didn't understand me and I didn't understand him,' she'd told him during one session. 'He was handsome, charming—and a serial philanderer. His whole life was based on what people thought of him. I was the less-pretty daughter, a socially awkward geek, so I was an embarrassment—at least until Pete made me famous. Daddy tried then, but by then it seemed too late. I didn't trust him not to hurt me. But now I—I wish I had given him another chance.'

It had been so hard to remain silent at that point. She was so beautiful to him—could no one else in her life see her as she really was? Were they all so blind that only fame made such an extraordinary woman acceptable to them? But he knew from bitter, silent experience that she had to lance this poison festering in her or it would warp her, change her from this incredible woman he loved, so he'd held her and let her speak without interruption.

'I remember some nights when I was little and he didn't come home all night. Mama would wait beside the front windows, waiting. She'd send me to bed, but when I'd get up to use the bathroom she'd still be there, watching for him. When he finally came home, usually in time for breakfast, she'd fuss over him, feed him and talk of something else, like nothing happened—like he hadn't spent the night with another woman. Like he didn't have her smell still on his skin. And when he went to work she'd go too, but she'd be wiping tears as she pulled out of the drive.'

Shuddering, she'd pulled away from him as she'd finished, but when she'd huddled into a ball by herself he'd dragged her back into his arms, rocking her until she sighed and gave in.

Her confidences had come to an end at that point, and he'd had more than enough to think about. Rachel was so beautiful, so loving and so wise, but she'd never been wise in her own life. Within a few hours of meeting her, she'd turned his world from hard and driven to the first true happiness he'd known since childhood. Something in him knew that, without his wealth or fame, she'd still think he was wonderful. Within a few hours of meeting his family, she'd healed decades of damage; they loved her as her own family didn't seem to.

Ah, was that it? Was that why she couldn't seem to heal her own hurts? Why she was so blind to everything he saw in her?

It was as if they stood on opposite sides of a slightly warped mirror, seeing the best and most beautiful in each other, but their own reflections were distorted.

He'd fallen asleep trying to work out what that meant.

As the captain announced breakfast, Rachel yawned and stretched so that he was obliged to release her. After the revelations in the night, he wondered if her movement had been deliberate, born of embarrassment or a need for distance from him. 'Are we almost there?'

It was odd. Just two days ago he'd have made a joke about that but now he felt unsure, as if he stood on shifting ground with her, even though she needed him here. 'The captain just said we're forty minutes out. We should get breakfast soon.'

'I really don't want to eat. My stomach….'

He smiled at her. 'I understand.'

'I'd better use the bathroom before we buckle up.' She slipped from the seat-bed and into the bathroom without looking at him.

She'd been doing that—avoiding his eyes—since telling him about her father's infidelities, and that she had been the unloved child. He frowned after her, but having no idea what to say or do to help her, he let it go. She had a hard day in front of her. His job was to smooth it as much as he could.

Armand was glad he'd organised a VIP private entrance to the States when he saw the media circus waiting for Rachel. From the customs stop to the limo was only a few steps and was so heavily guarded no one could approach her, only yell their questions from a distance—and as soon as they saw who was with her the questions doubled in noise and intensity.

'I never even thought about this, or that they'd know anything. I'm so sorry, Armand,' she sighed when they were inside the limo.

She was trembling again—and she hadn't faced the hardest part of the day yet. As the limo took off, followed by a varying assortment of vans, bikes and cars, he said, 'You didn't do any of this, Rachel. You have nothing to apologise for.'

'I should have known Pete would make a media announcement. Anything to gain a stupid sympathy bid with his fans.' Clenching and unclenching her fists, her gaze seemed fixed on her hands. 'I know you prefer privacy with—with your women—I mean, relationships. Just by your coming with me, I might as well have sold the story of being your latest squeeze to every magazine in America.'

Disturbed by the whiteness of her knuckles, he took her hands in his. 'Rachel, it isn't your fault. Let it go. You have more important things to deal with today.'

It was only when she sighed and nodded that he realised what she'd said.

Your women. Your latest squeeze.

Revolting words, yet it summed up his life until now with blunt vulgarity. And, combined with what she'd told him about her father, it was the most revealing thing she'd said since they'd first kissed. It switched on a light in his brain—but this wasn't the time or place to tell her that for all he cared the press could announce anything they liked if only she'd never say 'your women' or 'your latest squeeze' again, with that look of awkward embarrassment in her eyes. As if she expected nothing more than to be his latest lover, and be waved off like the others when he reached that exit door yet again.

Even their banter of yesterday took on new and dark connotations. She'd been putting a shelf-life on their time because of his past, and he'd played the game. He'd unconsciously confirmed that before long he'd want to leave her behind.

How was he going to make her recognise that

she was special, precious to him—that he loved her—when everyone in her life had used the words to get what they wanted from her? How could he make her believe in him when he still didn't know if he could be the man she needed, and when she didn't believe anyone could love her?

Within seconds of the security people ushering them into the house, Rachel felt a sense of sick fatalism. As she'd expected, Pete had got back ahead of them, and was in the centre of the family circle like a benevolent god. He was sitting right between her mother and Sara on the white leather sofa. Each of them sobbed on one of his broad shoulders and he held them with the tender affection of a long-accepted family member.

It was a photo op that couldn't be missed, and she'd be willing to bet it hadn't been. A quick sweep of the large, creamy-white living room revealed no strangers as yet, but she had no doubt they'd be there. Somebody from their network had to have been given the exclusive.

'Just remember, don't let him provoke you. No matter what he says or does, it's to make himself look good at your expense,' Armand murmured in her ear.

She nodded, holding tight to his hand. Even if he was only doing this to get Pete off-balance, she was grateful for the support.

Then her mother looked up and her ravaged face made Rachel forget all about Pete, his petty strategies for popularity, or anything else. Tears filled her eyes and overflowed. 'Mama,' she whispered thickly, and opened her arms.

Mama got to her feet and took a step. 'Rachel...' The look of bewildered grief was more than Rachel could bear. She ran to her mother and rocked her as Armand had done for her. Her mama held her as if she'd never let go, the most affection she'd had from either of her parents, except in public, since her wedding day.

To her surprise, it didn't feel awkward or guilty; it felt good, like coming home. 'Rachel, he's gone, your daddy's gone,' her mother sobbed. Rachel nodded, held her just as tightly, and they cried together, cleansing tears.

Before long Sara was there too and, beyond surprise that her sister wanted to be with her, Rachel made room for her. Poor Sara had always been her daddy's favourite girl and, given her nasty divorce from her husband, she doubted Philip would be coming to pay his respects or even to comfort his sons.

Sara's boys, Danny and Seth, joined the circle, demanding their place with loud voices. Only five and six, they looked frightened at all this grief. The poor babies didn't understand why their mother cried so hard she couldn't talk, and Sara was too lost in her pain to give either of her sons comfort apart from vague pats on their heads.

Rachel resolved to go to them as soon as she could, but right now her arms were full of her mama and Sara. She was almost relieved when Pete squatted in front of the boys and took them in his arms, murmuring the platitudinous explanations the boys were still too young to take in, but letting them know they weren't alone.

For the first time in Rachel's memory, her mama was a mess. She wore no make-up, her eyes were puffy and red, and there was dried tears on her cheeks. Her clothing was crumpled—her immaculate mother who got out of bed an hour before everyone else to dress, do her hair and put on her face. Now she didn't care, but Rachel no longer wondered at her mother's unquestioning love for a man who'd cheated on her too many times to count. She knew now that, despite any precautions against loving the wrong man, the man who'd never stay faithful, the heart still wants what it wants.

The thought made her turn her head a little. Armand was standing about five feet behind her, his gaze steady and compassionate, and yet with something sweeter and deeper as it rested only on her. He sent her a little smile, and amid her tears her heart sang just a tiny bit.

Funny, she'd never thought of herself as like her mother in any way until now—but she was definitely her mother's daughter. She was touched by joy amid her grief, because Armand was here. He'd crossed the world for her. And her heart kept right on wanting what it wanted.

Pete waited until after the funeral, when everyone but closest family was gone, to put his ultimatums—or was it simple blackmail?—to her.

She'd been right and wrong about the press. Pete had granted an exclusive to their network, of course, but only a short press release the next morning. Pete promised he'd handle it all without letting them get near Rachel, Sara or her mother. He gave the eulogy with simple, moving affection, the son her father had never had. Every time he'd gone home with her, Pete and Daddy had had a grand old time, fishing, drinking beer and talking sports.

Despite knowing everything he'd done was to lift his public profile as a sensitive guy, when Pete came to her room later that evening, she said, 'Pete, it was a wonderful eulogy, thank you so much—'

His interruption was brutal. 'Lose the boyfriend, Rachel. The network and media are expecting us to give a formal statement tomorrow about our reuniting.'

Rachel blinked once, twice, unable to believe his gall. 'You're blackmailing me the night of my father's funeral?' she asked, blank with disbelief.

He shrugged. 'It's your fault. I wouldn't have needed to resort to tactics that are beneath my dignity if you'd known your duty and come back with me from Europe.'

'You didn't even tell me my father was sick.'

He sneered at her. 'Why should I? You didn't call your mom to ask how they were. You didn't care about what I needed.'

Rachel gaped for a moment. 'You mean, I didn't fall for your lies again?'

He shrugged again. 'I said what women want

to hear. It doesn't matter if you're nine or ninety, all you women want the same stuff: *oh, you're so beautiful. I love you, baby, you're the only one.*' He mimicked the words with a withering look at her. 'I bet your current boyfriend uses them on you, too. It's the fastest way to get a woman into bed.'

Something went cold in her then, that he could be so callous after the moving tribute he'd given her father today. 'There's no use in trying to pretend we're back together, Pete, it will never happen. And there were a load of reporters when I arrived with Armand at the airport.'

'So? Tell them you're just friends. He helped you through our temporary separation. I've already told the network we're back together—and if you want that job in LA, I suggest you take the smart path and ditch the pretty boy. They want the perfect couple, not the cheating, deserting wife, to give advice on failing marriages.'

Rachel took a few breaths to cool her fury before she spoke; payback was the kind of childish vendetta she abhorred. 'What you told the press or our producers is your problem. You chose this path. You chose to play the pride card. You told the world that you left me for Jessi.'

His jaw jutted. 'You made that bed for me when you changed the locks.'

She sighed. 'I'm not going to indulge in any childish squabbles with you, Pete. I'm here for my family, not you. I owe you nothing now. You ended any obligation I still felt for you when you refused to take me to the emergency room after you broke my wrist.' She said it deliberately. He'd always skipped around the point, like it had never happened. 'I should have changed the locks after you broke my ribs.'

He paled, but with fury. 'You say it like I *meant* to do it when you *know* it was an accident, and you provoked me into it.'

She put up her hand. 'Stop blaming me for your violence, Pete. I won't keep enabling you in your delusions. I don't owe you your career, or your fame, either. You've cheated on me and hurt me more than once. Come near me again and the world will get those x-rays.'

'You just want to scare me,' he sneered. 'You wouldn't know how to be so disloyal.'

'You're right. I don't want to be disloyal, despite knowing you've been completely disloyal to me for the past twelve years, both in bed and with the show.' As his face darkened with threat, she added, 'Go ahead, Pete, just try to hit me. Even if we weren't in my mother's house, do you want to take bets that my big, protective lover is behind the door just dying for you to make the wrong move?'

Within a second, a tap sounded on the door, very soft, one only—letting them both know she wasn't alone.

Rachel watched Pete's gaze swivel to the door for a moment. His fists loosened, and she saw him for the total coward he was. Any man who'd only hit a much smaller woman, and only when there was no chance of his being hurt, wasn't worth fighting. 'I don't need Armand to protect me from the likes of you. I don't need you now, Pete. You don't love me, and I don't love you. I don't even *like* you. You're a cheat, a liar and a bully. You were lucky to have me for as long as you did.'

'You wouldn't have dared say that to me if your boyfriend wasn't here to give you courage,' he spat, shaking with what she guessed was the desire to hit her—the only way he could prove his dominance now he'd lost emotional control over her.

'Probably not,' she admitted. 'But it felt pretty good to say it anyway.'

'I don't like my lady being insulted, Rinaldi. I like it even less when a coward like you tries to intimidate or threaten her.'

As Pete made an odd squeaking sound, Rachel glanced at the doorway. Armand filled it with his darkness, with flashing eyes and clenched fists, like an avenging angel. One step in, and he was towering over Pete, who suddenly seemed small. Was he cringing?

'You're a pathetic piece of work, to put this on Rachel while she's grieving.' Armand spoke slowly, almost glittering cold. 'You will not speak to Rachel again. You will not insult her, hurt her or make empty threats, Rinaldi, because mine are *not* empty. If you touch Rachel again I will break a lot more than your wrist. I'll make sure your face is no longer pretty enough for TV—and then I'll destroy you.'

The words seemed so much fiercer for their being quiet and controlled. After a long moment in which Pete neither moved nor spoke, Armand added with cool contempt, 'I'd leave now if you want any chance of resurrecting your career. You have ten seconds, Rinaldi. Close the door on your way out.'

Without even looking at Pete again, Armand glanced at his watch. Pete scuttled out without a word, squeezing past Armand with white face and terrified eyes. The door closed quietly behind him. The click felt definite. A door closed.

As he looked at her, Armand's eyes softened. 'Are you okay?'

She nodded, feeling awkward. 'I'm sorry about Mama being so cold with you today. She believes marriage is for ever, and to have two divorced daughters…'

She felt the sentence trailing into emptiness and opened her mouth to speak.

His hands touched her shoulders. He smiled down at her, giving her space and comfort at once. 'Don't defend her, Rachel, there's no need. She needs to be angry at somebody right now. I don't mind it. My shoulders are broad enough.'

'That's so typical of you—you always say the right thing. How can you be so perfect all the time?' she burst out suddenly, losing it without warning. 'Don't you ever say stupid things, or get angry or shout, or want to hit…?' Then her foolish mouth stumbled to a halt when she saw the bleak look in his eyes.

'Yes, I do. But I have no urge to hit a woman, or a child,' he said with a calm too practised to be real.

She pulled away. 'What are you doing here with me? Was it just to be for me what you weren't for your mother, Carla and Johanna?'

His jaw worked for a moment but, though his fists clenched, he released them, slow and steady. He was pale, but his eyes burned as he looked at her. 'As I said, my shoulders are broad, Rachel. You need to yell at someone, here I am. Hit me if you need to. I can take it.'

'Of course you can, you're…' As fast as it came, her irrational anger dissipated—and far too late she finally understood. *Your father hit you long before you were twelve.*

She didn't need to ask. Of course his father had hit him. Small Armand, still a little boy, had taken the beatings so his mother and his sisters wouldn't have to be hurt—until he'd realised it had saved his family nothing. And, when he'd broken his father's nose in an attempt to stop the pain, he'd been sent away for his trouble.

Little Armand, only twelve years old, had been

sent to a boarding school far from home for the crime of trying to save his family from being hurt.

No wonder he'd crossed the world for her. Small Armand had been helpless to stop the abuse; Armand the man would never allow it again. And, because she wanted more than she'd ever have with him, she'd repaid his unrelenting care and healing by sticking a knife into ancient, unhealed wounds he'd refused to show the world.

Dysfunctional Rachel strikes again...

'Armand,' she whispered. 'I...' She floundered, looking at those eyes, so cold, withdrawn. Devastated beneath. The protective wolf fought for everyone else, but was still a wounded cub inside. Curling over the pain, he refused to allow anyone to see it let alone touch it.

She closed her eyes. In her need to lash out, she'd hit the one person who'd shown her nothing but care and loyalty. 'Armand, I'm sorry. I should never have...'

He turned away. 'I think I'll go for a walk.'

Then it clicked, and she knew what she had to do. 'Are you afraid you'll hit me if you stay with me? If I make you angry enough, you'll take a swing at me like you did to your father? Is that it?'

She asked it in deliberate challenge, waiting, watching, to see how he'd react.

He neither moved nor spoke. The stiff back and half-curled fists answered for him.

'Because I don't believe it,' she stated, softly taunting. 'You were right before. I don't believe you'd hurt any woman or child, no matter what provocation they give you.' Though she was pushing him, his stillness hurt her heart; she had to reach out, to touch him. Her hand curled around his. 'You are not your father's son, not in the way you fear most. You are a good, strong, wonderful man, Armand Bollinger. The only person who doesn't believe in you *is you*.'

Her hand fell from his when he pulled his away. He didn't turn back; he was still stood looking at the door. 'I didn't ask for your faith,' he said quietly. 'From the start, I've asked for nothing from you but an endorsement, Rachel.' And he walked out the door—that wretched farewell door he'd been watching constantly since the day they had met.

CHAPTER FOURTEEN

IT WAS so hard to find sanctuary when you were in an unfamiliar place.

When you could walk away from the woman who made you feel too damned much, who never knew when to stop pushing your buttons, but you couldn't make yourself leave her entirely. When it was the night of her father's funeral, she needed support more than she knew and she was surrounded by people who cared but were weak and defensive, who didn't understand her at all.

Go on, take it out on me. I can handle it.

The words came back to taunt Armand as he strode the streets of this upscale Austin neighbourhood, seeking solace in solitude, but what had always come before with ease now eluded him like a child playing hide-and-seek. Because this time he couldn't handle it, couldn't take the blows. Rachel needed him to be strong, to take her grief on his shoulders—but, even though her life was shattered and her future uncertain, her hits had come at him like knife blades in his solar plexus. Because Rachel was the one woman who saw past the barriers in his eyes as if they were open doors to his soul…and still she found something to like there, to desire. To Rachel, he wasn't the weak and shivering child he'd always known was there. The boy who'd failed everyone he loved.

What the hell did she see in him?

He heard the heavy breathing, the running steps and high-pitched whining gasps, and knew it wasn't an evening jogger.

'Rachel, give me some space,' he growled, increasing his pace.

One whine, another and another as she caught her breath. 'I need you, Armand. Please.'

The words were guaranteed to stop him in his tracks and, damn her, she knew it. But the grief lacing her voice wasn't feigned, and he'd already turned back before he'd made the conscious decision. 'What is it?' he asked, tense.

'I can't stay here,' she panted. 'I have to get away.'

Even in the uncertain glow of the street lights, he

saw she was trembling, could see the bewildered pain in her eyes. 'What did they do?'

'It's—it's so hard. I thought things might change after yesterday, but Mama's pressuring me to go back to Pete. She keeps talking about my vows before God being binding; Pete's playing the penitent-sinner card with her. And Sara...' She shook her head, looking at her feet, those shuffling feet. 'Sara resents me, because of you.'

Armand frowned. 'Me?'

'Don't pretend you don't know, Armand,' she said flatly. 'I saw the way she looked at you tonight, we all did.'

Yes, he knew. He'd seen the look in Rachel's sister's eyes tonight, after the wake had ended and the relatives and friends had gone home. It was as if Sara had noticed he was there for the first time—and she'd liked what she'd seen.

He met her gaze, shadowy with more than the night. 'And the famous psychologist would rather run away than deal with it?'

Her mouth pushed out before she spoke. 'That would depend on what you want in that area, wouldn't it?'

Something he'd eaten at dinner churned in his

stomach. 'I am not your father—or your ex. I've never cheated on a woman in my life.'

'Even if you want to,' she whispered. It wasn't a question.

'You said you saw her looking at me. Did you see me looking back?' he demanded.

She lifted her face, her smile holding more than the shadows beyond the moon's soft light. 'You're such a gentleman. Even if you wanted to, I know you wouldn't do that, not in front of my family. And it's not like we were really together. A few kisses, a bit of talk, really doesn't mean a thing.'

The shrug she gave was the most eloquent piece of nothing he'd ever seen, a tiny movement. It told him a story of a girl, a woman who'd never known faith in someone else, a girl whose best had never been good enough. She expected him to go. Even if he could tell her how he felt, if he could convince himself he was the man to make her happy, she'd never believe it, or at least not for long.

Just then, some words of Rachel's to Rinaldi came back to him: *I will not enable your delusions.* And he knew what he had to do. Just as she'd set his family free of their chains of pain and shame, he had to let Rachel go to find what she truly wanted. If he didn't, he'd never be more than her emotional umbrella, her place of hiding.

'I'm heading back home tomorrow, Rachel. I need to get to work on the third resort. I suggest you go to Los Angeles,' he said quietly, moving a step back so she couldn't see his face and understand the exquisite pain ripping through him. The sacrifice he must make for her sake.

'What?' The bewildered pain on her face seemed to bounce off the moonlight and streetlight like twin accusations, and the anguish doubled. *Come with me, spend your life with me and I'll protect you from everything that could possibly hurt you, including me.* Wasn't that what he did best, what he'd always done? And it was only now, facing the woman he loved beyond life or breath, that he knew it wasn't enough. Not for Rachel, and not for him.

'You forced me out of hiding, Rachel. You made me face my past, my weaknesses, and give my family what they needed. Now you have to do the same for yourself and your family.' He forced himself to sound expressionless when his entire body was aching to scoop her up and hold her, to protect her from anything that could hurt or upset her.

Or make her grow into a fully-functioning adult.

'It's time to stop running and face your life. Find out what you want and then do it, no matter what everyone else tells you to do. Go to Los Angeles. Meet with your producers, your agent and who-ever else has been pressuring you and tell them what *you* want.'

She shuddered. 'No, I won't. I can't.'

Stand still. Don't touch her, or give her an excuse to hide. 'You did it with Pete.'

'Because you were there!' she cried.

He put a finger over her mouth. 'It's always harder the first time, and even the second.'

Beseeching eyes looked up at him. 'Armand, please…not now, not this day.'

As the knife twisted in him, he realised some-thing, something big: she was playing him. Yes, unconsciously, she was using every trick in her psychologist's bag again but this time to make him give in to his wolf's nature, the need to protect, wisely or unwisely. He had to stop it, or those he loved would never become the people they needed to be.

So he turned his back on her, and those beautiful, drenched eyes that said *I need you.* 'Psychologist, heal thyself,' he said, forcing his voice to sound brutal. 'I might have chosen the worst day for this, but on any other day it will still be what you need to do. Go to Los Angeles and sort out your life. I'll see you when you come to endorse the resorts—but don't come to me unless you're the woman I've always seen in you. I want to see you taking charge of your life, being the woman who knows I'd never want to cheat on her and is ready to commit to a functioning relationship. A relationship without a shelf-life.'

'Says he who's always run through the first open door he sees?' she snarled.

'Yes, says that man,' he said quietly. 'But I'm not that man tonight. This is the man you made me. You made me stop running and listen to all that I denied.'

'You ran tonight.'

'No. I tried, but it didn't work.' Truth rang in his every word because as he said it he believed it. 'You've changed me, Rachel. I might have walked away tonight, but I can't run from who I am. And neither can you. I won't let you use me to become someone you're not, weak and clinging to me because you're afraid to face the world.'

He didn't say it, but they both heard it: *I'm not Pete.*

'What if I don't know who I am?' she asked, her voice thick.

'The woman who changed my entire family within hours knows exactly who she is,' he said with finality. 'The woman who took over my home and changed my life was comfortable with herself before I met her, and after. She didn't change herself to impress me or meet the expectations of others, and I respected her for that. That's the woman I kissed, the woman I want a relationship with. The woman you lost within minutes of walking into your mother's house.'

Her voice was wobbling, drenched in misery. 'And you think I'll find her again in LA?'

She gave that adorable, vulnerable sniff. Armand had to curl his fists into hard balls to stop from turning to her, snatching her close and telling her he'd make everything all right. 'If not there, then somewhere else. Either way, I hope you do, Rachel—because, if you don't, I don't want you.' He sounded so damned harsh, but there was no choice but to say it, now he'd begun on this, the worst night he could possibly have chosen to attack her. 'I want to be with the woman I knew in Switzerland. Rachel Chase isn't a weak and dependent woman. She's as strong as she is fragile, as beautiful as she is self-deprecating, and she's as honest with herself as others. She doesn't need me to take on her fights while she hides. She can fight her battles and she won't doubt my fidelity. She'll know I'll be there for her when she's done, win or lose. She'll know she's the only woman I want. If you can't be that Rachel, then I release you from the endorsement; don't come back to me.'

In the sounds of her tiny snuffles, he recognised and accepted that he'd made her cry and he hated it. Longing to hold her, he stayed with his back to her. It was the only way.

Then there was a long silence, and he hoped she was thinking it through.

It took about two minutes to realise he was alone. She'd left without a sound.

Rachel had walked away from him this time, and he knew that by the time he found her mother's house again she'd be gone.

The wait was on. He just hoped he hadn't pushed

her too far, that she'd come back to him—because he didn't know how many days or nights he'd be able to stand wandering in emotional darkness without her smile, her laughter and her touch to bring him to life.

Six months later

'So this is it, folks. I'm signing off from *Lifestyle Choices* on a weekly basis, though I will be hosting the occasional special.' Rachel smiled at the crowd of adoring fans' faces surrounding her and then at the camera. 'Look out for the first of my *Lifestyle Choices* later in the year. Good night, and remember—' she grinned as everyone in the audience chanted her mantra out loud '—if you don't love yourself as you are, nobody else will either!'

She laughed and waved as the camera went into fadeout. She spent another hour signing autographs and talking to members of the audience, many of whom were regulars begging her not to leave, that *Lifestyle Choices* was their favourite programme.

But she was done with fulfilling everyone's dreams but her own.

'Great show, Rachel,' Andy Sykes, the show's

executive producer, walked her to her dressing room. 'I saw the preliminary specs. This one's gonna rate through the roof.'

'Then hopefully the first special will too, Andy. But if not, I won't cry.'

'You know, if you want…'

Rachel smiled. 'I don't want, Andy. No more contract talk. I'm happy with my decision.' Seeing his dejected face, she hugged him and kissed his cheek. Then she closed the door, and turned to finish the packing she'd begun before the show.

She had started packing long before the first *Lifestyle Choices* had aired. She'd lived the entire six months in LA half-packed. But the show was something she'd needed to do for herself, without her mama's approval, without Pete driving her on to success—and without Armand having her back.

Standing alone. *Psychologist, heal thyself.*

She'd done it, faced her life. She'd faced Sara even before she'd left Austin that night six months ago. 'Find your own man, Sara, and stop trying to take mine. I won't apologise for my life, or give up what I want to make you happy.'

And, in seeing Sara buckle and make a slightly resentful peace with her sister, Rachel had known herself for the first time—had known what she wanted and understood what she had to do. Armand was right. She'd had to be free to find herself, to know what she wanted, before she'd been able to make her own choices.

She'd flown to LA, and accepted a six-month contract for the show that became *Lifestyle Choices*, having three separate lawyers check the contract to make certain there was no clause to force her into staying. Despite unrelenting pressure from everyone around her, she'd made a calm announcement on the first show that she was divorcing Pete, that they'd never reconciled, and that they never would. If people wanted her advice, it would be from someone who wasn't perfect, who'd made mistakes and wrong choices in her life. But divorcing Pete wasn't one of them.

That show, as Andy had just said, had rated through the roof, and tickets to be in the live audience had sold out for the entire season within hours.

Throughout the six months, she'd ignored all questions regarding her relationship with Armand, and refused all demands for disclosure from the press and the network.

During the whole time, she'd utterly refused to see Pete. Rejected by the network, he'd had to settle for a cable show that had fizzled within weeks. When it had failed, he'd inundated her with flowers—but when his calls, compliments, insults, threats and demands had bored her, she'd changed her address and phone number. When he'd come to the studio, she'd had him thrown out. When he'd tried her family, she'd gone to court, facing him as she'd got a permanent restraining order. The x-rays and doctors' report had come to light, and Pete's name became mud in LA.

Last she'd heard, he'd been pounding the pavement trying to sell his latest idea for a sitcom.

She'd faced each of her mother's tearful calls with the dignity she'd never known in her family life. 'Mama, I never loved him as you loved Daddy. Pete broke his vows, not me. I have no desire to forgive him, and less to have him in my life. If you want a relationship with me, it will be on my terms.'

After three months, she'd got her divorce certificate, and had barely restrained herself from throwing a 'freedom party' on the show, but her glowing face had said it all. It hadn't even shocked her when her mother had had her to Sunday dinner with Sara and the boys that week.

The dinner had been surprisingly pleasant, no guilt trips, no demands. Sara had found a new man. Bill Manning wasn't a doctor, wasn't a rich man or famous in any way, but he made her happy—in fact, Sara was glowing. Bill had come in time for dessert, and Rachel had liked him immediately. His quiet sense of self would be good for Sara.

As she flew back over the lights of LA that night, she had a silent epiphany. Freeing herself from Pete and her sham of a marriage, from family expectation and the feeling of never being good enough, had set her free of the shadows of the past. Thanks to Armand. And she realised how much he'd denied his very nature to give her this priceless gift.

And she loved him more than ever, ached for those nights they'd never had.

But now, she was free of all her obligations. She'd done everything she'd set out to do, and she'd done it alone. It was time to go to Armand—and hope it wasn't too late.

CHAPTER FIFTEEN

'THAT was very good, Rachel, but I really think that if we try just one more take we could make it perfect.'

Smiling that impish, sparkling happy grin, an immaculately dressed Rachel shook her head at the director and began pulling out the hair extensions that were so famous. 'Sorry, Manfred, but you see I don't do perfect.' Those shimmering eyes turned to Armand in cheeky challenge. 'What about you, Herr Bollinger? Do you want the perfect endorsement?'

What he wanted couldn't be expressed in public, but it must have been almost pathetically obvious that he was dying to get Rachel alone. Armand hadn't taken his eyes off her for a second since she'd arrived in Geneva by jet this morning, and everyone knew it.

Except maybe Rachel. If she'd noticed, there hadn't been a sign. She had been sweet, adorable, funny and professional all day. Her mind was on the endorsement.

'I think the last take was excellent, Manfred, thank you,' he said, striving to sound even. 'Ms Chase is right. We don't need perfection, and the light's beginning to fade.'

Here, Armand's word was law. Manfred sighed and muttered about edits, but accepted defeat. He called to pack up.

Armand strained to hold in his need as he walked over to her trailer. Inside, she stood pliant while the stylist removed the last of the hair extensions, scolding her for trying to do it alone, and the make-up artist removed the layers of paint needed for the cameras. Then she turned her face half an inch to be in his line of sight. She gave him that tongue-in-cheek smile and winked at him, and his body went into hyperdrive. He'd had to walk away before he snatched her into his arms and kissed her senseless.

All day she'd been the Rachel he wanted, the Rachel he'd demanded she become. It was driving him crazy to be so close, but never alone with her. Was she punishing him for asking too much? She didn't seem tense or angry; there was no yearning in her eyes, only sweet teasing.

Was she over him? Had she only come here for the damned endorsement?

Then, hours later it seemed to him, she emerged from her trailer, her pixie-cut hair back to normal wearing the jeans and trainers she preferred. She was *his* Rachel again—right down to the T-shirt that read, *sometimes your knight in shining armour is just a jerk in tin foil.*

He wanted to make a joke of it but then, wondering if it was a hint, he held it in.

'Shall we?' he asked quietly, pointing to his car, and she nodded.

They walked to the car in a silence that whispered 'awkward'.

'It's even more beautiful here than I remembered,' she said at last, her gaze on the valley, the Alps rising behind in spring-time beauty. 'How is your family? How is Claire? I'd love to see her. Is she at home?'

The warm tone made his heart pound. 'Everyone's fine. They all sent their love and want to see you too. Johanna and Carla came with their families when I said you'd be here. We can go see them now, if you like.' He added with difficulty, 'They're real fans of your show. They all watch it every week.'

'I'd love to see them.' They reached the Range Rover and, though he moved to hand her in, she jumped up herself. 'I'm so glad they like the show—but they'll have to wait a long time for the next one. I've decided to go in a new direction.'

She pulled the door closed. Taking his cue with a heart filled with uncertainty, he walked around the car and got in. 'Care to share what that direction will be?' he asked far too casually as he drove down towards the gate of the almost-finished resort. 'You never mentioned it on the air.' He'd watched every damned show, drinking her in, jealous as hell of everyone who got to see her, to talk to her, to touch her. He wondered every show if she could give it all up, if she'd ever come to him or if he'd have to swallow his pride and demands and go to her. He'd wondered if he could ever tell her she'd set him free. He was *not* his father's son, and her speaking that fear aloud, telling him of her faith, had been like letting a non-existent monster out of the cupboard.

He'd been on the verge of booking a jet to go

to her, with visions in his head of needing to beg her forgiveness or seduce her into coming home with him, when her agent had called to say Rachel wanted the endorsement set up. She'd be in Switzerland within a week.

'No. I didn't want the world to know.' Rachel stared out the window, drinking in the view, the alpine flowers dotting the landscape and lush grass. She spoke as if from a distance. 'I want to open a series of domestic-violence shelters and provide support for women and kids who feel they have nowhere to go, no one to listen to them or care. I was wondering if your mother or sisters would be interested in helping.' She turned to him, but her smile seemed remote. 'As fellow survivors, I think we'd have something valuable to give.'

It was like another hit to his solar plexus—but, as ever with Rachel, it was a correct hit, making him a better man. Sincerely, he said, 'I think they might do it. I think it's a wonderful way to use your best talents, Rachel. It's a brilliant idea—and I'd like to invest in it as much as you need.'

'Thank you,' she said quietly. 'But I was also hoping you might be interested in talking to the boys, the brothers and fathers? They'll need healing too.'

It was so tentative, that question, but without hesitation he answered, 'Yes, I would.' In fact, again it felt so damned right he wondered why he'd never thought of it.

It seemed he still had room to grow. He'd just needed Rachel to show him the way.

In the silence, he glanced over at her and saw the tears shimmering in her eyes: big as Texas, big as her heart—but was that heart his? He had to know. But he'd pushed her away, he'd made her do all these months of work, he'd set the demands in place. Now he had to wait for her to be ready to say what she felt.

'Thank you,' she said very softly, but as if she was thinking of something else.

'Are you okay?' he asked, feeling concerned. 'You've been working hard all day, and you must be so tired—jet lag is no joke. Do you want to rest?'

All of a sudden the unreal calm left her. 'No, I don't want to *rest*. I didn't cross the world for sleep. I want...wanted to tell you... Oh, darn it, Armand.'

This was it. Heart pounding like he'd run a race, he pulled over to the side of the road, just outside the village, and cut the engine. Looking at her, he saw her legs jumping up and down, her hands twisting around each other.

'Just say it, Rachel,' he said softly, lifting her chin, looking into eyes that weren't cheeky or challenging, but fragile, with wishes unuttered. 'Tell me what you want.'

Her gaze fell. 'Armand, I want… I hope that you still… Oh, drat it, I think I'm in love with you,' she blurted out, as if she hated every word.

As if she hadn't handed him the world all at once.

'You *think* you are in love with me?' he teased, his heart soaring. *She loves me.*

Her brow deepened in a frown. 'Look, I wanted to give you an out, if you only want a temporary thing with me.' She bit her lip, sniffed twice.

'I see,' he said gravely, holding in the laughter of pure joy. 'You *think* you are in love with me? It's really not good enough, *mon doux*. Either you are or you're not.'

At that gentle challenge ending with the endearment, her jaw jutted and her eyes flashed as they met his. 'You're not saying what you want,' she pointed out. 'You're not saying if you want it.'

'I know one thing. I don't want you to *think* you might love me.' He restrained the grin at the indignant look she shot at him. 'I want you to be brave, *mon coeur.*'

'All right, then.' With a determined look, she spilled out words. 'I'm crazy about you. I love you, I'll always love you, and I'm here for as long as you want me, all right? When you want me to go, I'll go, but I won't want to leave you ever. Okay? Did I say it right that time?'

She said it so fast, as if she was afraid she'd never say it at all unless she did it in a bunch. Armand didn't dare laugh yet, but the champagne bubbles of happiness were rising so fast he could barely contain it. As declarations of love went, it was the most aggressive, funny and ridiculous one he'd ever heard—but nothing had ever meant so much to him. 'It's all perfectly clear now,' he assured her with a quivering mouth. 'So you'll go when I say?' he added, pensive. 'But…what if I don't say it? What if I want…for ever?' As he spoke, he reached into his pocket, brought out a little box, and opened it.

Rachel gasped at the lovely, clean-cut diamond engagement ring and its mate nestled together. 'Armand…?'

'What if I say you're the most wonderful thing that ever happened to me?' he went on, taking the engagement ring out. 'What if I say you changed me and made me a happy man who's no longer afraid of commitment or of being his father's son? What if I say the last six months have been like a bleak wasteland without you and I never want to live another day, another hour, without you?'

Rachel sniffed again, but her eyes were twinkling. 'I'd say that all sounds lovely, but not quite romantic enough.'

At that, he burst out laughing. 'That's my Rachel. So, shall I say *I think I love you*?' he taunted, his eyes dancing.

She punched his arm. 'I'm waiting,' she said pugnaciously, but that adorable, big radiant smile was spreading across her face, lighting the car, lighting his life once again.

He couldn't help it; he kissed that inexpressibly kissable mouth and felt the rightness of it here in his mother's family village. History was repeating itself in the most beautiful way…a centuries-old tradition carried on and begun in the same moment.

Replete, and yet craving more, he pulled away an inch, kissed her again and then spoke. 'I've never said these words to any woman. I thought I never would—and then I met you. I'm crazy in love with you, Rachel Chase. I have been for months, and I always will be. I want you to be my wife, the mother of my children. I want to build a home here with you, raise our family and grow old—together; always together.' He held up the ring. 'Will you do all that with me?'

She was sobbing now, hiccupping breaths, but she stammered, 'Yes, yes, *yes*!' She only waited long enough for him to slide the ring on her finger before jumping at him, but she was restrained by her seat belt and fell back with a jerking movement. 'Oh, trust me to ruin my big romantic moment,' she grumbled.

Giddy, heady with the happiness only she had ever given him, he laughed. 'Ah, my adorable Rachel, I've missed you like crazy. Don't ever change, and don't leave me again.' He undid her belt buckle and his, and she jumped a second time, landing with a breathless thump in his lap.

'I never thought I could trust a man again,' she whispered between frantic kisses. 'But then there was you, my knight.'

'Sometimes I'll just be that jerk in tin foil, you know,' he whispered back, laughing. 'But I will always be *your* jerk in tin foil.'

'Mine for always,' she agreed, her eyes shimmering with love, and kissed him again.

And, even though the entire Bollinger family was waiting to celebrate the greatly-hoped-for engagement, they waited for hours with their champagne slowly warming and their balloons slowly deflating. They didn't get their hugs and kisses, or to start the party for a very long time.

But they didn't mind at all.

* * * * *